Caroline Blanche Elizabeth Lindsay

Bertha's Earl

Vol. I

Caroline Blanche Elizabeth Lindsay

Bertha's Earl
Vol. I

ISBN/EAN: 9783337039950

Printed in Europe, USA, Canada, Australia, Japan

Cover: Foto ©Andreas Hilbeck / pixelio.de

More available books at **www.hansebooks.com**

BERTHA'S EARL.

"Oft would I think, O Lord, what may this be
That Love is : of so noble might and kind
Loving his folk? And such prosperity
Is it of him as we in bookès find?
May he our heartès setten and unbind?
Hath he upon our hearts such mastery,
Or is all this but feignèd phantasy?"

James I. of Scotland

BERTHA'S EARL.

A Novel.

BY

LADY LINDSAY,

AUTHOR OF "CAROLINE."

IN THREE VOLUMES.

VOL. I.

LONDON:

RICHARD BENTLEY AND SON,

Publishers in Ordinary to Her Majesty the Queen.

1891.

BERTHA'S EARL.

CHAPTER I.

Miss Millings was the owner of a small house and studio.

There are studios and studios. London, perhaps more than any other city, teems with salient contrasts of many kinds—in her buildings as in her people—contrasts which result in much beauty or much ugliness, great luxury or exceeding squalor. It is not surprising, therefore, that the decoration of artists' studios should be a matter of distinction and difference. Foremost in our minds stand those palatial apartments connected

with many a pleasant afternoon of talk or
music—marble halls and gilded domes, wondrous shrines of art and antiquities, where
every available corner is hung with velvets,
draperies, and "stitcheries." On the other
hand, we are equally interested in some
severely simple and silent haunts whose bare
plaster walls are scrawled over with charcoal
memoranda—sketches for future pictures, or
addresses of models—and where the furniture
consists chiefly of easels, on which the works
in progress blaze like posies of coloured
gems.

There is no rule for a painter's work-shop ;
it is not always a question of expense, but
often of taste, and the surroundings of each
worker must please himself, and himself
alone. Before long, the walls become those
of his own castle, nay, of his own kingdom—
a happy impregnable haven where, un-
molested, he dreams dreams and sees visions.

And, whilst to one painter his luxurious home and its picturesque suggestions are absolute necessaries for the success of art, another, possibly a yet more ideal mind prefers to compose his colour-poem within such quiet greyness—mere absence of decoration—as neither defines nor obtrudes itself upon the imagination, but leaves each phantasy free scope to extend its wings.

Meanwhile, between these two extremes are to be found many pleasant sanctums, neither over large nor exceeding small, not splendidly filled, nor totally unadorned. Therein, busy toilers of various degrees of talent and energy labour on, ever happy in their future pictures, and as surely unhappy in their present ones.

Miss Millings, for the best of reasons, had not been lavish in the decoration of her studio. It was fairly comfortable nevertheless, and of moderate size, possessing a high

north window which admitted a vast amount
of brown London light, a sofa, some easy
chairs, a writing-table and a piano, whilst a
deep Dutch fireplace at one end formed the
chief feature of the apartment. A certain
number of studio "properties" were usually
scattered about: such as Japanese fans, a
quaintly carved Indian stool, a mandoline,
an ivory cabinet, a few broken specimens
of gaily-coloured Tuscan pottery, and some
faded silks and antique dresses, heaped on
chairs or screens in picturesque though
untidy confusion.

Opposite the fireplace hung a large and
ragged piece of tapestry, whereon several
faintly-discernible classic personages in impossible heroic attitudes appeared to be
eagerly following the most inexplicable
occupations.

It was a chilly February afternoon. The
firelight had triumphed altogether over the

waning and foggy light of day. A huge pile
of coal and wood blazed in the big chimney,
and red reflections went dancing about the
room, merrily lighting up the tapestried
personages, and exposing the faulty or
"scamped" portions of sundry pictures with
as slender pity as the critics would doubtless
presently bestow. Above all, the fire-gleams
shone ruddy on the faces of two girls who
sat together on the hearthrug, employed in
toasting muffins. Or rather it should be said
that Bertha Millings, a fair young lady of
five or six and twenty years of age, whose
hands were idly folded in her lap, was merely
watching and superintending the efforts of a
hoydenish though graceful damsel, considerably her junior, on whom the entire labour
of toasting had evidently devolved. The
toaster knelt, and swayed about, half-sitting,
half-balancing herself on her heels. She
was armed with a long fork, and seemed

well accustomed to her present occupation, and deeply desirous of fulfilling it satisfactorily. Yet, every now and then, she turned tempestuously, and faced her sister, repeating with some annoyance :

" Oh, I wish, I do so wish you wouldn't marry him ! "

Bertha shook her head. Possibly, she was a strong-minded woman, for she wore over her dark woollen gown a very plain pinafore of blue cotton. Moreover, there was an odd look in her well-shaped face—in her warm brown eyes specially—a look that might mean decision or might denote self-will, and which was not altogether softened away by the æsthetic aureole of fluffy golden hair that encircled and almost shrouded her forehead.

" My dear little Agamemnon ! " she exclaimed at last; " I wish, for my part, that you would not always anticipate events.

Suppose that such events never take place! You positively run after Time to seize him by the forelock! And he has never proposed at all."

"Not yet; but he will," replied Agamemnon, with discontent. " Besides, he isn't Time. I wish he was, I do, and then you couldn't marry him."

" My dear, what absurd nonsense! Well, suppose I wish to marry him ?"

There was a pause. The young person interrogated tossed back the thick yellow mane that was tumbling over her heated face, shrugged her shoulders, and proceeded silently with the toasting of her muffin.

" Well, Aggie ? "

" Well ? "

" Why don't you talk ? "

" Why don't *you* ? "

" Oh, because I have nothing particular to tell you. I expected you— —"

"To say that I *want* you to marry him?
To go right away and give up all your
beautiful, lovely work? And for all our nice
delightful times to come to an end? Of
course I can't, Booffles, how should I? He
is perfectly certain to hate the whole lot of
us—by us, I mean myself and Jemima—and
we—that's me specially—have thoroughly
made up our minds to loathe and detest
him."

"I hope you will not loathe and detest
him, Aggie! If I really thought you meant
it—— But I don't. My child, he is very
kind. And he isn't ugly."

"Well, no, not exactly ugly, of course.
Earls never are ugly, I suppose."

"Oh, bother earls!"

"Why, that's just what I say. Besides,
he's past being ugly."

"Past being ugly?"

"Yes. Mrs. Weagles says he's sixty if

he's a day, and there's a book—that's what
Mrs. Weagles says—which is kept altogether
for the ages of earls."

"Oh, Aggie, what a child you are! But
he is not sixty, really; only fifty-seven."

"What *can* you want to think of marrying
him for, Booffles?"

Miss Agamemnon hereupon, gathering
herself up, bent upon her sister so bright,
flushed, impertinent, and sweet a face, that
Bertha could only laughingly kiss it, whilst
she herself blushed deeply.

"You're a foolish little soul, Aggie. Some
day you will understand all these difficult
questions better, perhaps."

"Perhaps!" answered the young philo-
sopher dryly. "And perhaps I understand
more now than you think. Well, here's your
muffin; it's a little burnt, I am afraid,
though. Now for the *burro*."

The child's lanky arm was already outstretched for the butter-dish, when there came a knock at the door, and she started.

"Speak of the earl," she murmured, "and—— Oh dear, oh dear, here he is!"

Bertha rose hurriedly to her feet and advanced a step or two, whilst Jemima, who was parlour-maid, factotum, and friend of the family all in one, loudly, but with some difficulty of pronunciation, announced:

" Lord Delachaine."

An elderly gentleman, tall and of spare figure, entered, after a moment's pause at the door. His hesitation, his precise almost angular manner, might have been mistaken for shyness, as he made his way slowly across the room, cautiously avoiding the bristling easels, and, as he did so, sometimes stepping back, and nearly tumbling into the large pie-dish which Aggie had judiciously placed on the floor in the very middle of the studio, preparatory to cleaning her sister's paint-brushes.

But Lord Delachaine was not shy. He speedily recovered his usual calmness and sedateness of deportment, and, as he shook hands with Bertha Millings, he said with a grave humility that was curiously like condescension :

" Forgive me ; your room is rather dark, and I am very awkward."

In truth, it was Bertha who appeared the more awkward and confused of the two, as she murmured her few words of greeting.

The earl bent his head slightly but graciously in acknowledgment. He seated himself in the chair which his hostess proffered him.

" I am most fortunate in finding you at home, Miss Millings ; I was afraid you were in the country. You had thought of leaving town, I believe."

"Yes ; I mean I gave it up, it is so cold—
so untempting—won't you have some tea?"
stammered Bertha, who felt unreasoningly
nervous.

"And muffins?" added Aggie, who was
not nervous at all.

"Ah! thank you," acquiesced Lord Delachaine, contentedly depositing his hat and
stick on the floor beside him. "But may I
be permitted? Can I not do the toasting
for you, Miss Julia?"

"No, thank you, I would rather do it
myself," replied the child, with a child's
directness.

"Aggie always does want to do things for
herself," put in Bertha apologetically.

"She is quite right; it is a good principle,"
said Lord Delachaine, with suavity. "My
grandfather was like that. I remember
quite well his telling me : 'never let anybody
do for you what you can do for yourself.'"

There was a pause. And then:

" Do you know, Miss Millings," continued the earl, " I have always desired, and yet never quite liked, to ask you something ? "

" You have ? "

" Yes. And I think I will venture now. Why do you call your sister 'Aggie,' when her name is Julia ? "

" Because—because I called her Agamemnon."

" For the same reason," said Aggie, coming valiantly to the rescue, "just for the very same reason that I have always called Bertha ' Booffles.' Don't you see ? "

" I see," replied the earl, taking this lucid explanation with perfect calmness. " It is an admirable reason, Miss Agamemnon."

As he spoke, his mouth moved towards one side with the slow and sphinx-like smile that was its usual muscular expression of amusement.

"But," continued Aggie, growing very red, "no one else calls me anything but Julia; *no one else at all.*"

"Oh, run along now, dear!" said Bertha, whose feelings were growing as painful as they were complex. "Do run away, and look after Jemima for me. Thank you, darling; here, take the *Graphic* with you. Of course I'll call you presently."

CHAPTER II.

THERE was a prolonged silence after Aggie's departure. Bertha's heart went pit-a-pat. Her little sister's searching questions, so crudely put, so difficult to answer, had gone far to shake her out of the curiously comatose state of mind in which she had indulged during the last few days. And Lord Delachaine's unexpected arrival had discomposed her yet further. Moreover, she never could get used to his odd precise manner. It was a mixture of stateliness, deference, and haughtiness, all combined, to which she was quite unaccustomed. It was so different to the manners of most of her other friends. It was so chilling, so distant.

Yet he must care for her; else, why should he trouble himself to come? Of late he had come very frequently. What a pity that Aggie did not take to him! She, Bertha, might do very much worse than accept him, if in truth he meant to propose! The mere idea sent a thrill of nervousness from her heart to her very finger-tips. What a curious proposal it would be, were it ever to come about! Meanwhile, Bertha seemed to feel tangibly the stillness in which she and her companion sat facing each other. Yet, the more she recognized the discomfort of the interview, the less able was she to regain her self-possession. As she sat, sipping her tea with scalding haste, wondering what she should or should not say, her little sister's words, disagreeably persistent, recurred again and again to her mind. She felt half-inclined to laugh, half-disposed to cry. Was Lord Delachaine really too old to be ugly?

Miss Millings glanced furtively at the spare aristocratic figure in the arm-chair before her. It was the very type of an elderly English gentleman. She noted approvingly—considering his age—his thin pale features, his high nose and deep quiet eyes, the clean-shaven face, the short iron-grey hair—hair that had surely once been inky black to have turned into so dark a grey.

Whether Lord Delachaine entertained thoughts of love or not, he was now apparently chiefly occupied in taking off his gloves, before wrestling with a huge piece of muffin that Aggie had placed before him. The gloves were pale lavender kid, stitched with black—a tight fit; but, as their owner pulled them off with slow deliberation, it was evident that he brought a quiet and calm decision to bear upon even the trifling acts of daily life. It pleased Bertha to mark this ; she scarcely knew why. But, presently, as out of the pale gloves came two long slender hands, colourless as wax, with their equally colourless and scrupulously clean nails, she involuntarily withdrew her own dirty little pink palm from the table, and hid it within its fellow on her lap.

The movement attracted Lord Delachaine's notice. Indeed, he noticed most things. But he only said :

" May I have another cup of tea ? "

Bertha started. The commonplace request broke the thread of her rambling dreams. It was quite pleasant to awake. She suddenly regained her composure and normal brightness.

" It is always such a comfort when men condescend to tea !" she said gaily.

" Ah, now we can have a good talk !" indirectly replied her visitor, as he leaned back in his chair, with every appearance of comfort and complacency. " I like a good talk, Miss Millings ; don't you ? "

" Yes, I do ; but I am a woman. Any form of gossip is supposed to be natural and delightful to a woman."

" Ah, that is scarcely complimentary ! "

" Whilst, however great a chatterbox a man may be, he never gets abused for it."

" I am not a chatterbox."

" No ! " said Bertha, who could scarce keep from laughing at the comical suggestion.

" And yet I like to converse."

" Then again a man—— " continued Bertha hurriedly.

" Well, a man ? "

" Most men seem to want to do something else when they talk, as though that were not occupation enough. They turn over the pages of books, or else they pace up and down the room—unless, indeed, they smoke."

" The conversational powers of your

friends must be at a low ebb. I should
think most people would like to talk to you."

But Lord Delachaine did not act up to his
pretty supposition, for he became silent again.
When at last he spoke, it was with some
constraint.

"We have had a good many pleasant
chats in this studio of yours, Miss Millings."

"Yes," answered Bertha. And then she
added mischievously : "Did you want to discourse upon pictures now ? I have found
a most excellent new medium ; there is white
of egg in it. It is a most interesting dis-
covery. Shall I show it to you ? "

"Pray don't. I understand nothing about
pictures ; nor yet about mediums. And I
find my ignorance bliss in these days of
universal knowledge, I assure you. Not but
what I am interested in all that interests you.
However, I am occupied just now with the
plentiful portion of muffin that kind little

Miss Julia prepared for me. By-the-bye, it sounds so pretty to hear you call her 'Agamemnon.' Agamemnon is so very, so extremely unconventional."

"Is it?" asked Bertha, somewhat flatly. "I have often been afraid it sounded only foolish."

"Not at all—not at all. I like what is unconventional. It is charming, very charming. Miss Julia is your only sister I think?"

"Yes. Oh, Lord Delachaine, she is such a darling! She has been all the world to me!" And Bertha impulsively threw out her hands as she spoke, and clasped them again with rapidity, almost upsetting the tea-tray in her energetic demonstrance. "Aggie has always been the greatest joy of my life," she continued more quietly.

"My dear Miss Millings!" said the earl encouragingly.

"Aggie is twelve years younger than I

am. We have been orphans, oh, so long! And she is such a clever little thing, a real woman in sense and quickness. I would rather take her opinion than—than the Lord Chancellor's. I really would!"

"I never had much conversation with the present Lord Chancellor," said Lord Delachaine gravely. "I knew his predecessor better. But I am sure that Miss Julia——"

"Oh, now you are laughing at me!" interrupted Bertha. She was apt to interrupt. (For indeed, as a learned professor once explained to the writer of these pages, women always interrupt; that is one of their gravest faults. They all talk at the same time, and pause for no answer, whereas men judiciously speak in succession. Nevertheless, even a professor must admit that the results of most arguments are precisely the same, whatever method be used in the conducting of them.)

"I should never laugh at you," said the earl slowly. " I admire and like you. It is because of your warm heart that I think so highly of you."

Bertha coloured.

" Are you not warm-hearted also ? "

" I can scarcely say; I hardly know. In our family, it is not the fashion to be impulsive. You see things go in families; don't they ? "

" I suppose so," answered Bertha, dubiously.

" And in sets. Oh yes, I am sure they go in sets," said the earl meditatively. Then, after a silence, he continued :

" My life has been so different to yours, my dear child. I have had no little Agamemnon to pet me, and cheer me on. Ever since I can remember, I have been John Francis Charles, Earl of Delachaine, a being in a responsible and generally annoying position. Born too late for my advantage

in these democratic times, too early for my
tastes, which are often in advance of my
years, I have had my hands full of business
ever since I was a boy. My holidays have
been taken up with dull county meetings, and
the management of property and agents,
whilst in London my name has headed a few
philanthropic or agricultural societies, and
helped to make up the list of dinner-party
guests chronicled in the *Morning Post.* And
my extravagancies have been nominal ; perhaps a quiet hack for the park, some parlia-
mentary handbooks for my speeches in the
House of Lords, and the evening paper I
usually read at my mother's fireside !"

"Ah, your mother !" interposed Bertha.
" I remember my mother so well ! She was
so good, so dear, so very pretty ! But I
can't bear to talk of her."

"Don't," said the earl gently. Then,
smiling his strange smile : " I can mention

my mother, however. She is an excellent
woman, religious and sensible. Yet we don't
hold quite the same views sometimes. You
understand, I am sure ? "

" I—I don't know."

" I feel convinced that you comprehend.
You have imagination, and I have often
remarked that it is the imaginative people
who possess most sympathy—they realize
life most strongly."

" That is true," said Bertha, pleasantly
conscious of unusually subtle praise.

The earl bowed.

" My mother and my sister Dosia have
lived their own narrow life so long that they
strengthen each other mutually in their
opinions. To them, the outside world means
nothing. But their opinions are not mine."

Bertha nodded acquiescence.

" Still, we differ only in little things, in
very little things," continued Lord Dela-

chaine hastily. Then he added, " I am afraid you would think ours a very dull house, Miss Millings."

" Should I ? " asked Bertha constrainedly.

Her visitor's measured explanations were making her distinctly nervous.

" I think so," he affirmed, in his ruminating way. He was, in fact, mentally revolving strange possibilities and potentialities, at the mere thought of which he began to smile that slow faint smile of his again.

" You have never been dull, Miss Millings, I suppose ? "

" Oh dear, yes! " replied Bertha heartily ; " I have been *dreadfully* dull, lots and lots of times, and so has Aggie. I am miserably dull when I have got a headache, or when there's a brown fog, or when I don't sell my pictures and I—— "

She ceased suddenly, unwilling to allude to her frequent financial difficulties.

Lord Delachaine earnestly contemplated his boots.

"I suppose we all of us have our dark hours," he said quietly. "I can't imagine being very dull in this room, however. Well, Miss Millings, I have been boring you with my own affairs ; let me become your disciple ; show me this new medium, and tell me something of the rival claims of ultramarine and vermilion. I want to study art for the next five minutes ; then, alas! I must go home."

CHAPTER III.

LORD DELACHAINE walked slowly homewards. He did not even, as usual, hurry to get out of the somewhat squalid neighbourhood, with its slum-like narrow dingy streets, which surrounded Miss Millings's abode. Despite the chilliness of the weather, he seemed almost content to dawdle. Once, he even paused for a moment to examine with apparent interest an organ-grinder and his monkey, a pair of beings from whom, as a rule, he would have fled in unconquerable dislike. A few minutes later, he seemed struck by the almost weird aspect of a gas-lit public-house, from which the lurid light, as from halls of Eblis, emanated with difficulty through the dense and murky atmosphere. Indistinct figures flitted by on the pavement; ghostly-looking vehicles came suddenly and sharply into sight.

It had been raining, moreover. Whilst Lord Delachaine picked his way with dignified composure betwixt the puddles, impertinent little street arabs made faces at him behind his back. But there was within his breast a buoyant cheering sense which neither passers-by nor street arabs were likely to guess at. He had not felt so blithe for years; he found that he was positively thinking of himself as young. Is it a blessing, or the reverse that, whilst the body ages without remorse, the minds of men and women both are ever ready to take freaks of rejuvenescence? If only others could see us then as we see ourselves!

Presently, Lord Delachaine emerged into a better-paved and better-lighted quarter of

the town, and neared his own home in
Belgrave Square. The way seemed suddenly
very long to him ; the London streets more
dark and chill than usual. He had buttoned
his great-coat tightly across his chest, for
the fog was singularly penetrating and unpleasant. Certainly, he reflected, Belgravia
lies detestably low. Thereupon, his thoughts
turned fondly back to the pleasant fireside
he had so lately left—that kindly atmosphere
wherein Bertha held gentle sway. The
warmth and picturesqueness of it had mounted
to his brain. He could not forget it. He
had himself grown strangely impulsive under
this new influence—positively confidential.

Bertha was wonderfully pretty and attractive ; a charming little goddess, far superior to
any other women he knew, whilst Agamemnon—with her affection for her sister, her
long lank figure, and childish ways—even the
severe Aggie seemed by recollection inexpres-

sibly delightful. (For indeed, when he had left that fascinating studio, Miss Aggie, tilting herself well over the balusters of the staircase, had bade him be careful to wrap his scarf thoroughly about his throat, as the weather was dangerous for some constitutions.)

"Dear sweet little things, the two of them!" ejaculated the earl as, with an increasingly jaunty sense of the happy hour he had lately spent, he smilingly took the latch-key that hung upon his watch-chain, and by means of that small weapon opened the big and heavy front-door, and entered the mansion of his fathers.

A mansion it was, for it assuredly possessed the back stair necessary for the appellation ; but, viewed by an ordinary spectator, it appeared a dreary place enough— something not very unlike a prison. To Lord Delachaine, the entrance-hall was naturally

too familiar in its details to invite comment;
he betook himself immediately to his private
sitting-room, the door of which opened into
the hall.   This room was scantily furnished,
and in sombre taste.   The hangings were
drab, the wall-paper brown ; serious-looking
tomes, that filled many shelves, had their un-
compromising aspect increased in severity by
a wire lattice that protected them from the
touch of frivolous intruders. A square table.
covered with newspapers, blue books, etc.,
another—a big one—for writing, with many
locked drawers, and a large circular chair, that
swung round and turned its back aggressively
whenever approached by the uninitiated—
these were the chief objects in the room.
On the writing-table lay piles and piles of
bills and business letters neatly docketed by
Lord Delachaine's own hand, a massive
silver inkstand, laden with old-fashioned
seals, and around it a portentous supply of

writing-paper, quill pens and red sealing-wax, whilst beneath the table a huge and empty waste-paper basket seemed positively craving for its daily food.

The room, though otherwise so cheerless, was fairly well lighted. A careful valet had poked the fire, and drawn the old drab stuff curtains across the high windows; likewise, he had placed on the writing-table a shaded lamp, and close beside it some newly-arrived letters.

Nevertheless, the apartment found to-night small favour in its owner's eyes. He pushed aside his letters with a vacant air, leaving them unopened. The transient phase of boyishness was certainly fast fading from him. His thoughts were still with Bertha. Consequently, perhaps, his own stately sanctum appeared more empty and far less comfortable than usual. He passed his hand over his brow dreamily, almost irritably, as though to drive away the scenes that haunted him. The effort was a vain, as well as a painful one; all the more vain because, though he could not cure himself of thinking of Miss Millings, neither could he recover his previous light-heartedness. He sighed and turned, leaving his own room, and went slowly upstairs to the drawing-room.

The aged countess, his mother, was sitting there in her usual place, reading a religious publication by the light of an old-fashioned unshaded globe lamp. Lady Theodosia, on a sofa at the other end of the room, was evidently extraordinarily busy, surrounded as she was by a perfect litter of notes and invitation-cards, circulars, and other documents, which she was carefully sorting, and building up into little heaps and bundles.

" How late you are, John !" exclaimed Lady Delachaine, in a feeble and querulous tone ; and, as she spoke, her pamphlet dropped from her knee to the floor with a quick aggrieved tap of its own. " Have you been at the club all the time ? "

" No, not this afternoon, mother."

" It has been such a dull day. Not a cat has come near the place. I really always do think that February in London is a mistake. I wish you would shut that door properly, John. Now you have set me off coughing again ! Ah, that's better ; thank you, dear," added the old lady, somewhat mollified as the earl drew a screen in front of the offending door, after he had gently closed it.

" I do believe you have been to see those artist people again," said Lady Theodosia, veering suddenly round on her chair. " You are positively sliding down into Bohemia, John."

" I am, at any rate, old enough to choose my own friends," replied the earl stiffly. " I am sorry I am late, mother," he added, after a moment's pause; "but I did not know you were expecting me. It wants a quarter of an hour to dinner still, and I won't be five minutes dressing."

"That Bond Street man came at six about the cabinet," said Lady Delachaine, relenting easily, "and I didn't know what to say to him. You understand those things so much better than I do, John. I thought that the piece of embroidery you bought the other day would look very nice over the straight bit at the back, if the cabinet is to stand out in the room as you and Dosia want."

"What! Japanese embroidery on a Louis Quinze cabinet! Why, what can you be thinking of, mother?"

"I don't pretend to settle anything, of course," said Lady Delachaine, slightly ruffled. "That's just why I wanted you to speak to the man yourself. If you had been at home—— . But of course there's no use saying any more about it. After all, the place will be covered with stuffs soon. In my day, curtains were put on windows and nowhere else. And as for crockery——"

"Is Miss Millings fond of embroideries?" asked Lady Theodosia, who was quietly nibbling the feathers of her quill pen.

"Oh, bother!" said the earl. "How you do go on, Dosia! Everybody is bound to refurnish a little nowadays. Why, this room really looks like a penitentiary!"

"You go there every day, John; you can't expect mamma and me not to be frightened."

"Frightened? Of what?"

"Of a possible daughter and sister-in-law."

"You might have a worse."

"Scarcely, to our minds. A woman of the people, a regular Bohemian."

"It is difficult to define the word 'Bohemian,'" quoth the earl meditatively.

"Miss Millings is a thorough lady. One of her uncles was in the Church; her grandfather was in the army."

"Oh, John, John!" said Lady Delachaine piteously; "you speak sometimes as though you had made up your mind."

"Without reference to us," added Lady Theodosia.

"I do not recognize your right to catechize me," said the earl quietly. "If I marry, mother, it must be to please myself."

"Oh!" exclaimed Lady Delachaine, with a little jump. "John, my dear son, tell me the truth; have you proposed to that dreadful woman?"

"I have not proposed to any one," replied the earl, his face darkening.

As he made this remark, he recollected suddenly that Bertha had mentioned her comfort in Aggie's affection as a thing of the past rather than the present. Was it indeed

possible that the child held only a *second*
place in her mind ? That was a delightful
thought. Then he continued aloud and
defiantly :

"If by 'that dreadful woman' you mean
Miss Millings, let me assure you, mother,
that you are completely mistaken in your
estimate of one who is in all respects charming, and whom I consider to be in every way
my superior."

"John !"

"I think we need pursue the subject no
further," said Lord Delachaine, who had
risen, and now made for the door. His
hands were visibly trembling, but his figure
was exceedingly upright. "I am sorry that
I must dine at my club to-night. Good-bye,
mother. If you knew how it pains me to
hear you talk like this——"

"Oh, you are very unkind !" cried Lady
Theodosia, with increasing emotion; "you

are very, very unkind to both mamma and me. What have we done to you that you should take up with this commonplace stranger and treat us as you do, because we can't endure to think of her? No, stop, stop!"—for the earl had already left the room, and his sister was literally as well as metaphorically pursuing him—"stay; you *must* answer me one thing. Are you going to propose to her? Do you really think of making such a person your wife?"

"Good night, Dosia," said her brother coldly, wending his way rapidly downstairs.

This had been in truth a painful scene; yet, as he hastened along the pavement, it seemed as though his mental position were clearer than before. The weather had generously changed for his benefit. The fog had suddenly lifted, and the air was pleasant, almost balmy. His mind, likewise, was more cheerful and at ease. The remarks of his mother and sister had unintentionally exercised a bracing effect upon him, and had actually hurried him to a healthful decision. He was no boy to be coerced, he thought; no waverer needing guidance. He must be allowed to follow out his own ideas of happiness. Consequently, he would propose to Bertha Millings on the following morning; there was no time to be lost. What if such a treasure were to be secured by any other than himself?

But did she love him? What if she should refuse him? She was certainly unworldly enough for anything. She had not the rudiments of worldliness in her little finger! No, she was one of that rare sort who marry for affection only. Then, did she care for him, or did she not? This puzzle occupied the earl's mind until he reached his club; it fatigued his thoughts during his solitary dinner, and forced itself between the para-

graphs of mournful prophecies in the conservative evening gazette which he endeavoured
to peruse.   It even haunted his chilly walk
home, and hovered over his pillow during
the long and weary sleepless hours that
followed.

CHAPTER IV.

THE earl took Miss Millings by surprise on the following morning.

It was barely eleven o'clock when he was shewn into her studio. She was hard at work, painting from a dirty little Italian child, whose large black eyes, unkempt hair, and sullen expression, by no means suggested the angelic infant Samuel which she intended to represent. But, as Aggie had remarked with truth, if the subject failed as Samuel, it might easily be changed to an infant Hercules, or even an infant Christopher Columbus meditating on future discoveries.

The entrance of Lord Delachaine caused

some commotion in the studio. Bertha
coloured, painfully conscious that her hair
was not tidy, and that her hands were more
than usually covered with turpentine. Aggie,
engaged in household needlework at the
farthest end of the room, was hastily summoned to remove the youthful model, which,
on seeing the earl, immediately gravely
clutched its own right toe, and rolled over
into an unconventional attitude such as might
have made the fortune of any ambitious
painter, but was unappreciated by the be-
holders at this particular moment.

However, Aggie's strong lanky arms bore
down upon the poor baby, and she carried it
off in triumph, though sorely against its will.
Screams were heard, lessening in tone, if not
in continuity. The earl, meanwhile, had
walked up to the fireplace, and stood gazing
into the red embers, and turning his back to
every one. This, for him, was no little

rudeness. But he was, in truth, greatly pre-
occupied, and scarcely knew what he was
doing.

Bertha had, at first, cast terrified and
appealing looks at her sister; but the latter,
without returning her glance, hurried so
quickly from the room with her burthen that
the elder sister found herself alone with
her visitor before she had time to prepare
for the momentous *tête-à-tête*.

Time passed. Aggie, who dismissed the
juvenile model—having fortunately found its
mother loitering in the street—went upstairs
presently to hang out of a window which
commanded a good view of the entrance
door in hopes of shortly seeing the earl
depart upon his way. Here, after a long
while, she was discovered by Jemima; poor
Aggie's hopes were not realized, and Lord
Delachaine was paying a most unconscion-
ably protracted visit.

"Wasting all the good beautiful light, too," thought Aggie; "and there's not a breath of east wind to-day, and not an atom of smoke in the air!"

A darker thought than smoke clouded the child's heart; but she tried to cast it from her, at least until suspense should have become certainty. Yet it made her sigh; and Aggie seldom sighed.

"Lor! how you be a-dangling of your legs, to be sure! You'll be out of the window and on to the pavement in no time!" exclaimed Jemima, coming into the room, with a duster in one hand and the butcher's book in the other.

The sight of this well-known shiny red volume brought to Aggie's mind a great complication of difficulties.

"Suppose Lord Delachaine stays to lunch, Jemima!" she ejaculated.

"Well, suppose he do, miss?" was the

phlegmatic answer. "You don't need for to go and worrit your head about that."

"But I think Bertha would like me to," answered the child meditatively.

"Well, then, worrit if you please," said Jemima with sarcasm, as she began polishing the cover of the book with a corner of her apron. "We poor sinful creatures is all dust alike, and I've no doubt but what his lordship's 'ad to content himself with chops before now, and will again, miss, never you fear!"

Jemima's religion was of a distinctly gloomy kind.

"We're all alike, missy," she went on to explain, shaking her head ominously. "Lords and beggars, sinners every one of us, and whether by-and-bye we goes up or down——"

Aggie broke in, laughing irreverently:

"We'll have no need of chops, any way, Jemima."

That worthy woman, notwithstanding her

affection for the child, whom she considered her nursling, often had cause to shake her head reprovingly at Aggie's sayings. On this occasion she seemed deeply shocked as she retired from the room.

In point of fact, and despite her levelling tenets, she was hurrying to her kitchen, where she intended to prepare as elegant an impromptu repast as possible, in case Bertha should press Lord Delachaine to remain. For, as Jemima acknowledged to herself, without any twinges of conscious inconsistency :

"Earls is earls, and different to black-berries on a bush. Not that he's anything like a match to look at for Miss Bertha; but it would be better than them nasty paintings, anyhow, with a smell enough to knock you down, and a mess all over the place, and hard work—which it isn't lady-like—from year's end to year's end."

It would, indeed, have been difficult to satisfy Jemima's requirements for her favourite. Though she was fond of her younger charge, the elder was essentially her pride and delight. Bertha's grace and beauty appealed very strongly to the saturnine woman, who had no ties of her own, and whose rugged exterior and Calvinistic character formed so strong a contrast to the radiant nature of her young mistress. Fortunately, perhaps, Miss Millings was not to the full aware of her powerful sway over one who, seldom responsive, was sometimes even aggressively disagreeable.

Aggie remained tilted upon the window-sill for a considerable time. There were few passers-by, and the outlook was undeniably dull; still she remained. She had thrown a shawl—one of Bertha's studio properties—around her head and shoulders to keep herself warm. Despite this precaution, how-

ever, when finally her patience gave way,
and she drew in her head from the cold air,
she felt as chilled as she was sorely depressed.
Scarcely knowing where to go or what to
do, she left the room impetuously, and ran
downstairs. In the passage below she found
herself suddenly confronted by Lord Delachaine, who was really, truly, at last
departing!

He was alone, having already closed the
door of the studio behind him; he was
moving but slowly, almost standing still, in
fact, holding his hat and stick mechanically,
and gazing vaguely at the opposite wall.

Aggie, as she heedlessly advanced, bumped
up against him, inflicting a terrible blow on
that irreproachable hat. But Lord Delachaine did not seem to perceive the injury,
nor to resent the attack. There was something very odd in his manner; Aggie could
not but be aware of it instantly. As he laid

his disengaged hand upon her arm, she saw that his fingers were trembling. She looked quickly up into his face ; it was grave and dignified as usual, perhaps a trifle sterner in expression. He was surely pale; but his eyes were shining curiously.

" I am glad you have come back," he began, in an odd slow voice. "Will— will you say something to me ? " Then he added precipitately : " Bertha must tell you."

It was the first time he had called his hostess by that name. Aggie was instantly struck by the startling fact, and she looked at him yet more enquiringly. An icy fear encompassed her. She could not speak.

" She is to be my Bertha now," said the earl, very gravely. "Will you not wish me joy, dear child ? "

But Aggie remained as cold as stone. She made an effort to speak, but she could find no words. Her lips opened and gave forth no sound. At last:

"I—don't—know," she said, with a pause between each word. "Oh yes, of course I wish you joy, only——"

"Only what?" asked Lord Delachaine, almost eagerly.

"You might have married somebody else," said Aggie, staring fixedly.

She did not make the foolish speech rudely, but thoughtfully, as though she were contemplating the situation from every point.

"Yes, you might have married somebody else," she repeated, with melancholy certainty.

The earl let his hand drop from her arm. Surely, this reception from his lady-love's only relative was dispiriting. Nay, it was positively painful to him. He had cared, more than he knew, for the child's favour. He now felt more disconcerted than he had ever been in his life.

Aggie, too, was conscious of placing herself in the wrong. She did not know exactly how she had erred. Nor did she mind very much. If Lord Delachaine were wounded, why, so was she. He had attained all he wished for, whilst she had a perfect right to be bitter.

"Won't you let me pass?" she asked, in her hardest tones. "I think Bertha is sure to be wanting me."

"Oh yes, she is sure to want you," said Lord Delachaine dreamily.

There was evidently nothing that he could do. He stood aside in the narrow passage, and allowed the haughty little slender figure to pass without another word.

Then, somewhat forlornly for an accepted suitor, he made his way to the door, and went out into the street.

Meanwhile, Miss Millings was truly, as Aggie had foretold, "wanting" her little sister.

In all the trials and troubles besetting her
lonely life during the last few years, Bertha
had unreasoningly relied on that plain-spoken
young counsellor, claiming, even when not
actually asking or accepting counsel, a loving
sympathy which was never withheld. For
the child had been ignorant, as children must
needs be, of much that affects or grieves
grown-up folks, and her fresh and tender
affection had often comforted Bertha, proving
that kisses and happy prattle, and the clasp
of two warm energetic arms, can sometimes
be more efficacious to soothe and cheer than
tons of worldly wisdom or cart-loads of
sensible advice.

But to-day it was different. For the first
time in her recollection, Miss Millings had not
only passed over much gratuitous advice from
Aggie, but had positively run counter to it.
She herself was not sufficiently in love with
the earl, perhaps, to cast all care and thought

aside and make herself perfectly happy in the contemplation of a visionary future.

It is said that no right-minded woman ever really acknowledges, even in thought, the full amount of her affection for a man until he has definitely proposed. I am afraid that the history of all times and all countries is a strong witness against the truth of this assertion. Women may perforce keep silence until betrothal, but luckless indeed is the wooer who does not read the language of his lady's eyes before he asks the momentous question! The earl's proposal left Bertha more scared than happy. She had partly, if not quite expected it; yet, even as people allow themselves unreflectingly to drift into many a dangerous stream, she had always been willingly blind to the possibilities of the future.

Even now that the asking and accepting were over and done, there seemed something

unreal about the whole scene just past.   It
appeared odd to Bertha that she was not
more delighted, that her heart, in fact, was
utterly numbed and unstirred.   She did not
pause to consider how, at some of the most
critical moments of our lives, we realize only
faintly what is taking place.   Nor was this,
perhaps, in truth, now genuinely the case.
Her feelings—except those of passionate
love, which were altogether untouched—
were very tumultuous, even jarring.

Above all, her sense of responsibility for
her little sister's happiness assuredly at this
supreme moment more than counterbalanced
her desire to please Lord Delachaine.   For,
though she was conscious of the agreeable
thought that, as his wife, she herself might
be both secure and happy, whilst also able
to procure many advantages for Aggie, this
consciousness was embittered and almost
overpowered by the reflection that the *soli-*

tude à deux which she and her little sister
had cherished as to everyday events, and still
more with regard to inward communion,
must now be destroyed, never to be taken
up again.

For the first time in her life, Bertha feared
to meet the child's innocent courageous eyes.
Aggie would read the truth too easily, would
be inconveniently inquisitive. Her unso-
phisticated questions might be disagreeably
searching, her grief—if, indeed, Aggie should
give way to grief—more painful than anything that Bertha could imagine. Therefore
it came to pass that, after Lord Delachaine's
departure, the elder sister did not instantly
call the younger, as was her wont when
alone. She busied herself with putting her
brushes and colours in order, convinced that
she could paint no more that day. As she
took the canvas of the infant Samuel from
the easel, she gazed thereon curiously before

turning the sketch with its face to the wall.
What a step she had taken during the last
two hours !　The paint was still wet on the
rosy mouth she had been portraying, but,
since she had laid on that careless touch of
madder, she had promised Lord Delachaine
to be his wife, to give him her thoughts, her
ambitions, her affection, her very existence.
The painted child's smile was unmoved ; the
work, good or faulty, had in nowise altered ;
but for Bertha Millings the whole world had
changed.

This particular picture was destined never
to be finished.　In the future to which she
was now tremulously looking forward, there
came to the painter a day when she again
held the canvas in her hands, and gazed
earnestly upon it, the sight of it bringing
back (as a drawing, or a perfume, or a bar
of music can so vividly bring back) the old
associations, the old studio, the old life, and

the old sense of wondering and bewilder-
ment, whilst she herself seemed again to
stand in her old place by the easel—Bertha
Millings, who had just pledged her troth to
the ninth earl of Delachaine.

When Aggie finally came into the room,
she entered noisily enough, her head high,
her cheeks flushed.

"So you are going to marry him, after
all!" she said, in a voice that, to Bertha's
nervous ears, sounded extraordinarily harsh.

Recciving no answer, Miss Aggie began
to wander about the studio, straightening
the position of some china pots, which
Jemima, according to her usual custom,
had placed carefully awry on shelves and
cabinets.

"I should have thought he was too old
to know how to propose!" she went on
aggressively. "I wonder how he managed
to begin! Tell me, did he say, like the man

you once told me of: 'Dearest, call me *plain
John* ' ? "

There was an almost ferocious glare in the
child's eyes as she threw a quick glance over
her shoulder at her elder sister. Bertha
remained standing, perfectly motionless, her
hands tightly clasped. It was to be even
worse, then, than she had expected!

"Aggie !" she murmured appealingly.

"If it had only been Dr. Jackson," continued the tormentor, lifting up and putting
down with a bang a plaster cast of an
unoffending Diana. "Why," she repeated,
" *he* thinks of nothing else in the whole wide
world but you. Now, *he* would have known
what to say."

"You think so ? " asked Bertha, somewhat
scornfully.

"Well," continued Aggie, "you will go
and live in your castle with your wretched
old earl, and I shall be sent to school."

"No, no; I have already arranged about that."

"Well, then, I shall go and be Aunt Barbara's slavey, or live with Jemima at the seaside, while you start off on your honeymoon to Paris, and Florence, and Vienna, and —Carthage, and—and—and Seringapatam."

Aggie's voice broke a little at these last words. She was standing in the middle of the studio, her face flushing more and more. Suddenly, with an expression of the deepest pain, she began to tremble all over; then she threw out her arms towards her sister, and ran to her, kneeling and crouching at her feet, and pressing closely up to her as she burst into a passion of sobs.

"Oh, Booffles," she sobbed, "oh, forgive me, forgive me!"

And Bertha broke down also, and the two foolish creatures, crying piteously, lay close in each other's arms.

At last, raising her tear-stained face, Aggie spoke.

" Darling, will you promise me one thing ? "

Bertha nodded.

" Well, if—if the time ever comes that I'm away from you, Booffles, and got ill, very ill, that's to say, would you leave everything and come to me at once ? "

" Why, of course," answered Bertha, a little surprised.

" Suppose," continued the child uneasily, " suppose your earl were very ill too ? What would you do then ? "

" I don't know," answered Bertha ; " please don't think of anything so terrible. If he is my husband, I suppose my first duty will be to him ; don't you see that, dear ? "

She clasped her little sister very closely as she spoke. It was evident that, as she was not yet married, duty and inclination might still go hand in hand.

" That's a very disagreeable thing to think of," said Aggie.

" Is it, dear ? "

" Very !   However, he mightn't be so ill, and if he wasn't, you'd be sure to come ? "

" Sure."

" You promise ? "

" Promise."

" You swear ?   Oh, Booffles, do swear."

"Very well ; I   swear, then," answered Bertha, half-laughing, half-crying.

Aggie gave a contented sigh.

" I've always thought," she said, " that it would be almost quite nice to be ill, just ill enough, you know, yet not too ill— or even if I were dreadfully ill, it would make it better, you understand—to have you on one side and Dr. Jackson on the other."

To this remark Bertha made no reply. She buried her face in Aggie's fluffy mane.

" I think he does care about you," con-

tinued the child sententiously; "indeed, I
am sure of it—your old earl, I mean."

"Oh, do you, darling?" ejaculated her
sister joyfully. "Tell me why; dear little
Aggie, tell me why!"

"Because," said Aggie, somewhat shame-
facedly, "I tried him yesterday. I put a
taste, just a wee little bit of a smear of
turpentine on the corner of his muffin, and
he ate it all up quite contentedly. Now, if
he hadn't cared about you, Booffles, don't
you see——"

"Oh, you bad child, you very naughty
child!" exclaimed Bertha, who was really
horrified.

But at this juncture the door opened, and
the two girls started to their feet, as Jemima
announced:

"Dr. Jackson."

CHAPTER V.

DR. JACKSON entered. He was a short thick-set young man of about eight and twenty years of age. His step was quick and energetic, his eyes were quick and bright, and he spoke quickly, as indeed he did most things.

"My dear Miss Millings, it is unpardonable to disturb you at this time of day—I know your laws are those of the Medes and Persians—I never dreamt of it, believe me—it was my friend Jemima who persuaded me—I called at your door for a moment to ask when I might see you—she told me you had sent away your model, and were not working."

"Indeed, I am quite idle," answered Bertha, who was too accustomed to her visitor's idiosyncracies to be surprised at the rapidity of his disconnected speech. " I have left off work for to-day altogether."

" Really! What, with such a light ? "

Aggie, painfully conscious of red eyes and a generally tempestuous aspect, had already made a hasty escape. Bertha, though gracious in word, turned her back upon the new-comer. She was not wont to trouble herself to bestow much civility of greeting on one whose own courtesy was habitually scant. The young man, in nowise disconcerted, followed his hostess across the studio, and settled himself down by the fireplace in the very chair wherein Lord Delachaine had rested his limbs but a short time previously.

It was impossible for Bertha, even in her present perturbed mood, not to mark the difference between these two men. Yet, though youth was on his side, the doctor was not especially good-looking. His hair and eyes were dark, his face exceedingly pale; his teeth were perfect, but he scarcely ever shewed them, not because, like the earl, his lips seldom relaxed into a smile—nay, he talked and laughed nearly as much as he gesticulated—but because his mouth was hidden by a bushy moustache and beard. He was powerfully built, with broad shoulders and strong square hands. This manly strength of aspect saved him from ungainliness, for power has a grace of its own; nevertheless, the shortness of his stature deprived him of any claim to elegant or artistic proportion.

We all cherish a secret vanity, and the size of his biceps and the breadth of his chest were regarded by Dr. Jackson as his most inestimable merits. Even his scientific capacities were not so gratefully contemplated by himself. But his friends, who appreciated his physical gifts less warmly, liked him chiefly because of his deep soft voice, and a certain sympathy of manner which, with all his off-handedness, bespoke a lurking tenderness that called around him every beast, bird, child, or human being in need or distress.

Dr. Jackson's patients—for though a young man he already boasted many—were well aware of the kindness of heart that underlay his brusque speech, and they often traded upon that kindheartedness.

"Well, what have you to say to me?" asked Bertha, leaning back in her chair.

She had suffered from such great tension of nerves during the whole morning, that the prospect of a quiet chat with this sympathetic friend was an absolute relief. He was indeed her greatest friend, and, next to Aggie, her favourite confidant. For, as she frequently told herself, Edward Jackson's benevolence took the place of other people's tact, and it was almost a charity to lay a

slight share of one's own burthens and vexa-
tions upon his cheerful broad shoulders.
Consequently, the doctor habitually listened
to many a piteous tale of financial difficulties,
chilling anxieties, or—occasionally—eager
professional hopes. He had become such a
fidus Achates to Bertha that she took up a
great deal of his valuable time without the
slightest compunction. Needless to say, he
had been witness to the ardent commence-
ment of nearly all Miss Millings' pictures,
and had followed their career with deep,
though unlearned interest, often wishing
that he might become the writer of leaders
in the *Times* to extol their merits, or a rich
city merchant to purchase them freely. Oddly
enough, however, she had never mentioned
Lord Delachaine to him, except very casually
and carelessly. There had not, as she always
said to herself, been really much to mention
—as yet.

In return for Dr. Jackson's advice and
help, Bertha's soft womanly ear had many a
time hearkened to the recital of the young
man's own efforts, of his courageous battling
with difficulties and poverty, and recently of
his rapid rise in his profession—rapid considering his youth—all expressed with the
ardour of much faith in the future.   He had
no mother and no sisters.   His fairest ideal of
home was that quiet corner in Bertha's studio,
where the firelight gleamed and flickered on
the frames of her pictures, and lit up the
ragged tapestry.   His spare minutes were
chiefly those of twilight, and the darkness of
London, its fog, or intermixed rain and snow,
made the warmth and light within but the
more appreciable.

Of late, certainly, when he had called in
the gloaming, he had occasionally been told
that Miss Millings was engaged.   Once,
indeed, he found Lord Delachaine sitting

with her, but that nobleman's manner was
so courteous that the younger man, who had
but few dealings with the aristocracy, and
imagined that an earl must be the very best
buyer of large oil works by rising young
artists, became himself unusually unobtrusive
and polite.   Nay, on that solitary occasion,
Dr. Jackson bade his hostess the quickest
possible farewell, and was not a little dis-
appointed afterwards to find that Lord
Delachaine had neither ordered a full-length
portrait, nor desired the immediate removal
to his own house of that large composition of
Ruth and Boaz which had hung fire so long.'

Despite the fact that Dr. Jackson was a
rapid talker, on this present occasion he
seemed to deliberate as carefully before
giving utterance to his thoughts as even the
earl might have done.   When at last he
spoke, it was by no means brilliantly, for he
merely said :

"How odd it seems, Miss Millings, for you and me to be sitting here opposite each other on a fine morning like this, idling and wasting our time!"

"Very odd," replied Bertha; "only, Dr. Jackson, I must draw your attention to the fact that it is not civil to call talking to me waste of time."

She smiled as she spoke. Any other day she would probably have laughed outright, but to-day there was a tightening at her heart which made even smiles difficult. She had not yet recovered from the emotion of her scene with Aggie, to say nothing of her interview with Lord Delachaine.

Probably, also, at any other time the young man would with alacrity have responded to her attempted banter, but to-day he quietly ignored it.

"I can't think what fellows do with stupid wives," he remarked irrelevantly. "To my thinking there would be nothing so delightful as a woman who worked at home all day, whilst her husband went out."

" So as to see as little as possible of each other, do you mean ? "

" No, no, of course not!" answered the young man impatiently. " You see, I have come to talk seriously to you, Miss Millings," he went on, after a moment's pause ; " to ask your advice, in fact, and you don't make it easy."

Bertha started. Was it possible that her friend, like herself, contemplated matrimony ? What a curious coincidence ! She was touched.

" If I hurt you by talking nonsense, I am sorry," said she, strangely humble ; " I have asked your advice, Dr. Jackson, so often— oh, scores and scores of times—and you have been so kind, so helpful!"

There was a quiver in her voice as she

spoke, and tears came into her eyes. Possibly, Dr. Jackson misunderstood the cause
of her emotion, for he leaned forward in his
chair very eagerly, and began talking in his
usual rapid way, with an energy and fire that
needed no further encouragement.

"I will tell you. I have had the offer of a
very good practice away in Devonshire, not
far from where my father is living, a nice
cheery town, a comfortable big house, a view
of the sea—I know you like the sea, Miss
Millings; I mean, I'm awfully fond of the
sea myself, you know. I used to be there
ever so much when I was quite a little chap.
Of course it's not London! There's no
chance of quite—well, perhaps not quite the
same distinction; but I'm not a genuinely
scientific man, you see. I don't think—I
really don't think I'm an ambitious one.
Now, tell me the truth, do *you* think I am
ambitious?"

" I—indeed I cannot say," answered Bertha
thoughtfully. " Perhaps you ought to be
ambitious ; yes, I am sure you ought. Why,
when I come to remember, there was no
limit to what you meant to do. Surely, Dr.
Jackson," she added, once more trying to
be playful, " you intended first to set the
Thames on fire, and then put it out again by
means of some wonderful nostrum that you
should discover yourself."

" I don't know what I may have meant to
do," said the doctor, with a sigh, leaning his
face on his strong hands. " I suppose we
are all of us foolish when we are young ; the
only hope for a man is to get less and less
of a fool as he grows older, and I'm not very
old yet, so who knows ? I may grow to be
a Socrates or a Solon before I've done, after
all. You wouldn't care for me, Miss Millings
a bit the more, would you, if I were an elderly
fellow, with scanty grey hair and a thin face,

and a hesitating sort of a wrinkled mouth
that had lost all its sense of fun, and a new
shiny hat that shewed I had grown great
and prosperous and grand? Would you
like to see me taking particular care of my
gloves and umbrella, member of all kinds of
learned societies, with perhaps a baronetage
in prospect, and an old age of discriminating
and well-regulated comfort ? "

There was something in this picture—Dr.
Jackson could not guess why—which made
the red blood mount precipitately into Bertha's
cheeks. With an abrupt action of her arm
she threw down a book that lay on a small
table beside her ; her face was hidden as
she bent hastily to pick up the book. The
young man bent also, their hands met for
an instant ; then his soliloquy—for it seemed
almost to be one—took another turn.

" I told you I wanted your advice. I have
come to you for it, so please reflect carefully.

I mean to take your advice and yours only. Tell me what I shall do. Shall I accept this country practice, and work for—for happiness, or shall I stay here in my dreary little lodging, a votary of Fame, till I have climbed a few steps higher? Tell me, Miss Millings; tell me quickly."

" I tell you ?" exclaimed Bertha, turning very pale as the real meaning of his questions began to dawn upon her. " Oh no, no; I cannot tell you. You must decide for yourself, Dr. Jackson. Every man's life is his own making; his friends cannot interfere in it."

" His friends? No, perhaps not—that is, not his ordinary friends and acquaintances; but you have been, you are, far more. You —ah, what might you not be! Why, it is you who are yourself my life, even while you hold it, to break or to make. Bertha, Bertha, I have thought it all out. Only listen to me."

" No, no ! ' cried Bertha, trying to stop him ; but he would not be stopped. She had risen to her feet; he barred her path.

" Fame is nothing to me," he urged ; "nothing in comparison with what I plead for. Until to-day I have never dared to say anything—my lips were shut because of my poverty—it would not have been honourable otherwise—don't you see that it would not have been honourable ? I had nothing to offer you. I could not speak."

" Oh, do not speak now ! " cried poor Bertha, clasping her hands. " Oh, ¦ hush, hush ! We shall both be the happier if you have not spoken."

A change came over the young man's face. Something in the tone of Bertha's voice dis-illusioned him. He also had risen to his feet. Now he drew back a step, and stood staring in silence at his companion.

" I don't know what you will think of me,"

began Bertha slowly, and then she paused. Something seemed to rise in her throat which made her words inaudible. Then she took courage anew, and forced herself to continue:

"It will make me so dreadfully sorry, if I have ever said or done anything to give you unhappiness. Forgive me, oh, please forgive me if I have. I am engaged to Lord Delachaine."

She had been afraid to look up. She was fearful, though of what she scarcely knew.

No answer came to her avowal. The impetuous torrent of her friend's speech was surely checked now; yet his flashing eyes were fixed upon her with a look of keen enquiry; his pale face was even paler than before. At last he spoke:

"You have done it for Aggie's sake," he said.

His voice, though very gentle, was so

piteously altered that Bertha looked up hastily, scarce recognizing the sound.

" No," she answered, crimsoning deeply ; " it would not be altogether true to say that. I have done it for many reasons ; yes, for many, many reasons."

There was a long silence. The young doctor sat down once more, and buried his face in his hands. He sat mute and stunned. It seemed to him as though an icy blast were suddenly driven between him and the warmth of expected happiness. At this one stroke all his hopes were dashed to pieces ; there was such vividness in his sense of wreckage, that he almost expected to see the walls of the room wherein he sat totter and fall about him. Then swiftly the sensation changed. The whole world had grown suddenly blank and empty ; he did not want to go out into it any more. And his heart was blank and empty likewise, except that therein raged and swelled a fierce wave of indignation, that for the nonce ousted all tenderer thoughts. At last he rose to his feet; time was passing; was it morning or afternoon? He knew not; he only knew that he must go. And he spoke out of the bitterness of his soul:

" This is the first time that you have not chosen to ask my advice."

" Oh, do not say so!" pleaded Bertha tearfully. " Do not be angry with me! Indeed, indeed, I never knew that—that——"

" You never knew?" echoed the young doctor roughly, almost contemptuously. " Why, even Aggie knew! Ah well! I shall never hold the child on my knee any more now. It will be good-bye to the old friend-ships. As for you, Miss Millings, if things are as you say, we shall doubtless both be the happier for not explaining too much now."

" Don't go quite yet," pleaded the trembling

girl, laying her hand on his sleeve. "Oh, don't go, don't!"

"What should I stay for? Well, tell me one thing; are you happy?"

"I ought to be," she answered, drooping her eyelids; then, raising them as suddenly, she looked up with strange defiance. "And I am going to try to make Lord Delachaine happy; I ought to do that—you will say that I ought to, Dr. Jackson."

"I have nothing to say for or against it," he answered, turning away wearily. "How should I?"

The conscientiousness of her effort was assuredly lost upon him.

"Good-bye once more. You will scarcely need congratulations from me, Miss Millings; your friends will lavish them on you sufficiently, believe me."

"Oh, don't let us part like this!" she

exclaimed, following him. "Won't you say just one word of comfort to me before you go ?"

"Comfort ?" he ejaculated, almost with a laugh. Then, after a pause, he added more gently : " I will say this, just this. It will be better for us not to see each other any more—what have I to do with the Earl of Delachaine's affianced wife ? But remember that, if ever you want me, if ever you are in need or trouble, and I, from my lonely corner of the world, can help you—let me know. To me you will always be Bertha."

Here the young man's voice shook, and he turned his head aside. Was this really his last farewell to the fireside he so loved, to the woman he had so long adored ?"

"Ah !" he resumed, with a wretched attempt to smile. " There's no need to ask your advice now ! The house on the Devon coast may be given to the first comer for all

I care—London for me, and a draught of Lethe. Well, good-bye."

"Good-bye," said Bertha timidly.

He took her hand, and held it in his strong grasp. His face was pathetic in its misery.

"Good-bye, my dear; God bless you always," he murmured almost solemnly. Then, with quick strides, he crossed the room. Before she could speak again he was gone.

As Dr. Jackson passed out of the house he seemed to carry away with him an echo of Bertha's voice, half a sigh, half a whisper— a last farewell. Was it a recall? He neither stopped nor looked back, however. His strength of mind had been taxed to the very utmost degree. He was longing passionately now to leave this place, to return to the solitude of his own four walls.

He had shut Bertha's front door behind him, and had already begun to cross the road, when that echo was wafted to him again ; this time even louder and clearer than before. Then he stood still, and looked about him. In his present excited mood he could have believed anything possible— any vision, any phantasmagoria of fancy. Nay! there was no one visible. Why, he was standing in the very middle of the road, which, on every side, was quite deserted.

Again came the floating and mysterious "good-bye." This time he solved the mystery, for, looking up, he saw Aggie at an open window. She was gazing after him wistfully, her face softly framed in its masses of fair hair, some blue draperies protecting her from the cold.

In silence he lifted his hat, and waved it to the child. Then he ran on very fast. The little vision had given him a fresh pang of intense pain. He loved Aggie better than everything else in the world ; yes, everything—except Bertha.

CHAPTER VI.

THE remainder of that never-to-be-forgotten day passed heavily enough. Bertha was thoroughly disinclined for all work, being alternately listless and restless. Aggie made several heroic though unfortunate attempts to appear cheerful ; each one resulted in abject failure.

There was nobody in particular to whom the good news of Bertha's engagement need be hastily communicated ; hence both sisters were conscious of a flatness which is seldom felt under such circumstances. The orphans had indeed many acquaintances, but scarcely any relations, and only few friends. The old Aunt Barbara, to whom Aggie had impetuously alluded, was an elderly spinster, who dwelt in a secluded village in Yorkshire. She was neither as rich nor as generous as maiden aunts are usually supposed to be. She was extremely deaf, excessively ill-tempered, and she did not care to hold any correspondence or communication with her nieces. She considered herself deeply offended by the degrading fact that Bertha had become an artist. Had that young lady gone out charing, Aunt Barbara could scarce have been more irate. At the time of Bertha's choice of a profession, Aunt Barbara had indited and hastily posted many angry letters. These, at first lengthily responded to, had been gradually neglected, and left unanswered. As a natural result, since the installation of Miss Millings in the London studio, the rupture had been complete.

On the other hand, Mrs. Weagles who lived next door, though in nowise a relation, was a truly kind and affectionate friend.

Nevertheless, and despite an enormous dis-
crepancy of years, she was in reality more of
a companion to Aggie than to Bertha. In
the eyes of the latter, Mrs. Weagles was
but a commonplace uninteresting old lady,
too fond of gossip to invite much confidence.
Thus it was that Miss Millings, even whilst
she bethought herself of the fairly numerous
circle who invited her to dinner, or who
joyfully flocked to her tea-parties on Show
Sunday or other festivals, could not call to
mind any choice spirit to whom she specially
longed to rush and unburthen herself of the
great news. Aggie and Edward Jackson
had been so continually the recipients of her
confidence that she had hitherto felt the need
of none other.

As for Jemima, that trusty and faithful
retainer was speedily made aware by Aggie
of the earl's proposal; but she received the
information with her usual mysterious severity.

"Wants to marry Miss Bertha, does he? Well, well, there's no knowing what may fall on any of us, any day. Peer or pauper, we're sinners every one alike—man is but a fading grass, all travelling in the same direction."

"Are you glad he's got a lot of money, Jemima?" asked Aggie, intensely desirous of shifting the responsibility of expressed satisfaction on steadier shoulders than her own.

"Eh, Miss Julia," came the chilly answer, "'God help the rich, the poor can beg.' I'm not one of those to speak again' authority. But I've heard it said as how 'a gentleman without living is like a pudding without suet,' and so maybe's maybe, and there's wiser ones than I who've found themselves in the wrong box before now, though 'Like to like, and Nan for Nicholas,' seems the more nat'ral way of the world."

"Bertha's as good as Lord Delachaine,

and better," began Aggie hotly, as she dimly guessed the oracle's meaning.

" Ay, ay, missy, that's the very nutshell of it. But he's one that gives no trouble, as I will say for him, wiping his feet as nice as nice on the new rug that lays outside, and it's a fine sounding name and a fine gentleman for his years."

Yet Aggie, as she stalked out of the room with her head in the air, was not satisfied ; nor did Jemima, to do her justice, for one short moment imagine that her well-selected words were likely to give satisfaction.

The afternoon wore slowly on. When it was already late, Bertha declared her inability to remain any longer at home, and the two sisters wandered out without any distinct purpose. Finally, they chartered a hansom, and were driven to Oxford Street, where they walked for some time, amusing themselves by scanning the passers-by, and peering in at the shop-windows, until their spirits had somewhat risen. The flush of exercise mantled in the cheeks of both girls, and there were many who turned to look with admiration, and even smiling benevolence, at the two pretty faces.

Aggie, her rebellious mane tied into a decent plait, hung with clasped hands on Bertha's arm, expressing much pleasure with regard to the novelties of the season exhibited in the windows; but Bertha was naturally graver and more sober.

"Do walk straight, dear Aggie; do walk quietly."

The jewellers' shops especially attracted Aggie's attention, and she held forth on the subject of rings. She was specially delighted with a small ring representing two tiny forget-me-not flowers wrought of turquoise, with diminutive green enamel leaves on either side.

"Such a dear, sweet, wee little thing!"
she exclaimed. "Just what I should like
you to be given by somebody, Booffles. I
hate great, big, flaring, diamond sorts of
things, don't you?"

But Bertha, decorously uncertain of what
the future might hold in store, refused to
pronounce any opinion.

"There are rings and rings, you know,
Aggie," she said evasively.

"Oh, of course!" answered that young
damsel airily. I only know what I should
like, if I were you, and—and——— By-the-bye,
Booffles, what am I to call Lord Delachaine?
You won't be hurt, will you, darling, if I say
—I mean, if I think—he really is a great
deal older than I am, you know?"

Aggie's explanation was only calculated
to make matters worse. In truth she had
dropped unexpectedly back into the burning
question. She had not intended to be again

flippant on the subject of her future brother-in-law's age. But she was unaccustomed to conceal her thoughts. Through her foolish young mind flitted sundry diminutives befitting an affectionate relationship; but these all seemed equally unsuitable. "Chainie" and " Dellie" would surely be pert appellatives, whilst "Johnnie" was certainly out of the question! Yet she did not wish to say anything that might hurt Bertha's feelings. The elder sister, meanwhile, turned her head slightly away.

"Take care of that omnibus, Aggie—now we can cross. I think you had better go on calling him Lord Delachaine, dear."

"All right!" answered Aggie, immensely relieved. Then, child-like, she immediately flew to another train of thought. "I forgot to tell you, Booffles, that, just before we came out, I was playing in the garden, and Mrs. Weagles beckoned me into her house. She

was what Jemima calls ' all of a twitter ' ; you
know what I mean, dear, don't you ? She
said she had guessed the wonderful news,
and was ever so delighted. She considers
the earl quite one of the grandest-looking
people she has ever seen. I thought you
would like that; but, somehow, I forgot
about it. Then she said our positions would
be a great deal changed. Will your position
be changed, Booffles ? "

" Yes, darling, I think a little," said Bertha
gravely.

" But mine won't ? " asked Aggie nervously.
" Mine won't, will it ? "

" I hope not, dear," replied the elder sister,
somewhat tremulously. " You are not going
to leave me, you know, darling ; and we
ought to try and think of all the bright things
—all the pleasant things."

"Yes," said Aggie, nodding her head ;
" I know what you mean. Mrs. Weagles

said they'd be sure to come and see you—
all the relatives."

Bertha passed over in silence this suggestion of pleasant things to come.

"Fancy all the good we shall be able to
do!" she said encouragingly.

"Shall we be richer?" asked the practical
Aggie. "Will you be richer?"

"I—I think so," answered Bertha hesitatingly.

"Not richer than if you had sold Ruth
and Boaz—at the catalogue price, I mean?"

"I really can't tell," said Bertha, with a
slight—a very slight—touch of asperity.
"It is getting late; we ought to be going
home, now. And do look where you walk,
Aggie! You have gone right into another
puddle!"

They reached home, tired but invigorated
by exercise. On the hall-table, Jemima had
ostentatiously placed a small parcel and a

note. The parcel—quickly opened—contained an extremely fine old-fashioned diamond and sapphire ring, that seemed positively to blaze into Bertha's eyes, and, by its magnificence, to illumine the dingy little entrance-hall like a shining star.

The note—a short one, eagerly conned by both sisters—was written in a small, precise, almost crabbed hand ; the wide margin and straight accuracy of the lines being very noticeable.   It ran as follows :

" MY DEAR BERTHA,

" Pray accept from me, as a token of regard and affection, a ring which belonged to my great-grandmother, and which I trust you will wear for my sake.

" Your affectionate

" DELACHAINE."

Bertha turned to look at her sister, but

the child was gone. Then Bertha slipped
on the ring with a sense of possession that
was decidedly pleasurable. She could not
help admiring the beautiful stones; moreover, it was certainly gratifying that her
betrothed had lost no time in making her
this first offering.

Meanwhile Aggie, as she fled upstairs
with burning cheeks, wished, in the sensitive-
ness of her heart, that the earth had opened
and swallowed her up before she had made
that unlucky remark respective of flashing
diamonds. Also, in her wilful spirit there
arose a jarring thought which was annoying
to her, though she could not give expression
to it aloud. Surely the earl might have
gone himself to a shop to buy something
nice and new for Bertha, instead of sending
her a nasty snuffy old ring that had been
worn by his great-grandmother!

Possibly, however, had Lord Delachaine

purchased a ring of the very latest make and design, he might still have failed to satisfy the requirements of one small critic of his acquaintance!

CHAPTER VII.

"I suppose we ought to go and see that horrid woman," said Lady Theodosia.

"I am afraid so," answered Lady Delachaine, with a sigh. "We must do our duty, Dosia. Of course it is no use for me to enter into details and explain to *you*——"

"Why, no, of course not," said Lady Theodosia pettishly. "Really, mamma, I know as well as you do that John has gone and done for himself, and that he won't find it out at once, though *we* may. After all, we ought to consider ourselves very fortunate that it didn't happen long before."

"Yes, my dear, I am sure you are right—there is always a bright side to everything."

"I meant that we ought to thank our stars the evil day was put off so long. Mothers and sisters go for very little in these things, mamma; and when a man once gets on the wrong side of fifty, he is sure to be led by the nose by some woman or other. And there are lots of dangerous ones about."

"My dear," interposed Lady Delachaine, "I don't think you speak quite—quite as you should. John is your brother, you know —your elder brother."

"Yes, he is my elder brother," admitted Lady Theodosia, with a short laugh; "and men have this advantage over women, that they can make idiots of themselves at any age."

"It is very sad," said Lady Delachaine, shaking her head, and letting her keys and needlework fall in a forlorn tinkling heap from her lap. "It is certainly very sad."

She heaved another long sigh, then spoke.

"Would you mind ringing the bell, Dosia, to have the fire made up?"

Lady Theodosia gave the bell a vigorous pull.

"Don't you think you had better order the carriage, mamma?"

Lady Delachaine gave a little start, which sent her pocket-handkerchief and gloves —she always carried gloves, according to bygone fashion—sliding down after the rest of her belongings.

"Do you think we really need go to-day?" she asked piteously.

"Certainly," replied her daughter with decision, stooping briskly to pick up the pocket-handkerchief and other items. "Here, mamma, are your things. Winslow, the carriage at three punctually."

"Yes, my lady."

"And the fire," added Lady Delachaine.

"Yes, my lady."

"Ah, dear, dear! it is very sad," repeated Lady Delachaine, patting her eyes gently with the handkerchief she once more held, and sighing so deeply that Winslow presently communicated to friends downstairs his con-- viction that the future bride must be a most undesirable addition to the family— judging by the appearance of the family ladies.

At three o'clock the barouche, with its big bay horses and ponderous accessories, stood at the door. The coachman, who had been five and twenty years in his present situation, and wore a wig, knee-breeches, etc., sat proudly on the box; the powdered footman was drawing on his gloves, and joking in an undignified way as he stood by the carriage, pleasantly conscious that his afternoon duties had not really begun, for the elder of the ladies of the house was never remarkable for her punctuality.

But to-day, exact to the minute, Lady
Delachaine rustled downstairs, her long
black silk robes (much betrimmed and fur-
belowed) flowing three or four steps behind
her. Stern Nemesis was behind her also, *i.e.*
Lady Theodosia, in a tightly-fitting tailor-
made suit that was rather short in front,
whilst the plain bonnet, firmly fixed upon her
smooth hair, as well as the double-soled boots
that frankly peeped from her skirts, seemed
to be constantly repeating : " no nonsense, no
nonsense."

Lord Delachaine, after the manner of men
in difficult positions, had absented himself
for the whole day. He had much pressing
business on hand—so he had stated at an
early hour, as he swallowed a hasty breakfast,
during which meal his mother shed intermit-
tent tears, and his sister glared stonily at the
tea-urn.

On the preceding evening he had worn all

his best arguments thoroughly threadbare;
he had endeavoured to melt his mother, but
she had not melted in the special manner
that he wanted. She had clung to him
damply, begging him to take pity on her.
As for Lady Theodosia, she had summed up
her feelings in one terse sentence :

"You are old enough to know your own
mind, John, and so I trust you will have
no reason to repent ; but, as you did not
choose to consult us in this matter, you
cannot expect mamma and me to say much
about it."

"You have said quite enough," retorted
the earl, turning at last. Then, for he
honestly desired to be a peace-maker, he
added : "I am sure you will like her,
Dosia."

To scorn and entreaty alike, however,
Lady Theodosia had deigned no reply, and
the earl's pride kept him silent forthwith.

Some days had passed since the announce-
ment of the engagement, before her future
mother and sister-in-law proposed to visit
Miss Millings.   They had no tangible cause
for such disapproval as would have allowed
them to remain away altogether.   On the
other hand, it was quite unnecessary to
evince undue haste, which might easily be
construed into approval.

On the present alarming occasion, Bertha
sat anxiously expectant.   That morning the
earl had called, and she had spent an hour
of pleasant conversation with him ; but neither
his mother nor his sister were mentioned.
Bertha had praised the diamond and sapphire
ring, and expressed her gratitude.   Lord
Delachaine, as was but just, had praised the
finger on which the ring had been bestowed.
When the betrothed pair presently bade each
other a smiling good-bye, Lord Delachaine
announced his obligation to pay an immediate

visit to his lawyer, and departed in a sudden fit of hurry, promising to look in again during the afternoon.

It was only after he had left the studio that he seemed to recollect that there was something else to say. Then he reopened the door gently, poked his head in, and, startling placid Bertha with the following casual remark : "Oh, by-the-bye, my sister Dosia tells me my mother's probably going to call some time to-day," he disappeared as swiftly as he had but just reappeared.

On their way to the abode of the dreaded Miss Millings, neither Lady Delachaine nor her daughter uttered a syllable. They leaned back in the barouche, with that bored ex- pression which people usually wear when out for a drive. It has been argued in favour of the contentment of the poor, that folks in carriages are often seen to yawn ; but this is surely due rather to the swinging motion which induces languid contemplation and repose, than to the lack of such a happy heart as necessarily cheers the pedestrian.

But it was neither the mildness of the weather, nor the cee-springs of the barouche that evoked an expression of annoyed lassitude on the faces of these two ladies. They were thoroughly irritated—justly so, as they thought—with the world and the decrees of Fate. Nor were they soothed with regard to each other. Lady Delachaine considered her daughter unsisterly in her mode of speech; Lady Theodosia mentally characterized her mother's manner as absurdly limp and yielding.

When they finally reached the artist's home, they looked at each other enquiringly. Was it better or worse than they had expected ?

Jemima answered the bell. (There was, alas ! no knocker whereon the footman might exercise his skill.) It was Jemima also, who, in appearance rather red and almost as haughty as the visitors themselves, ushered them into the studio. After she had announced their arrival she departed, muttering to herself, as was her wont. She was greatly displeased by Lady Theodosia's general aspect, but she viewed Lady Delachaine with more indulgence.

"The poor body!" quoth Jemima to herself. "She's near her end. The young *may* die, but the old *must.*"

So saying, the worthy woman hurried off to communicate her impressions to Susan, who was factotum to Mrs. Weagles, and who, despite her youth and consequent new-fangled ways, was held in some estimation by solitary Jemima. But alas! for that good opinion. Susan, having hastily donned a most becoming new cap, had already started the rudiments of an interesting conversation with Lady

Delachaine's tall footman from her vantage ground on the steps of Mrs. Weagles' house.

Meanwhile, Bertha hurriedly rose from her sofa corner, and advanced with rapid steps to greet the new-comers. She looked very lovely in her pale grey gown with its clinging folds, her soft short hair pushed back, her eager face slightly flushed, and her eyes bright with that particular appealing glance which had dealt such an unerring stroke at Lord Delachaine's heart. But the hearts of some people's female relatives are by no means unprepared for the attacks of a pretty young creature of their own sex. With a momentary survey Lady Theodosia took in the whole situation, stigmatizing the ragged tapestry as pretentious, the velvet draperies as tawdry, the pictures on the easels as miserable rubbish, and the owner of the studio herself as nothing more nor less than a little minx. However, Lady Theodosia stepped forward briskly as usual, and, taking Bertha's trembling hand in her strong grip, she gave it a shake that positively hurt, whilst Lady Delachaine, flurried and nervous, could only vaguely stammer :

"Oh, my dear! We felt we ought to come and see you, you know. Is it really true? Are you going to marry my poor John? Oh dear, oh dear, you must talk to her, Dosia—this is Dosia, you understand. And is this really where you live? And do you paint all day? And is this your drawing-room? And don't the oil paints smell very nasty, and make your head ache? And are you obliged to stand? It's so bad for the ankles. There, Dosia, I've dropped my pocket-handkerchief again!"

Bertha placed the old lady on the sofa and sat down beside her; her own head— whether from oil paints or other reasons— was certainly in a whirl. She could think of absolutely nothing to say that in the very least befitted this momentous occasion. Lady Theodosia sat opposite, having chosen the high stool which was generally reserved for models, where she perched, like a long-legged bird, apparently uncomfortable and insecure, yet refusing to move.

Bertha, who was blessed—or afflicted—with a strong sense of the ridiculous, now began to feel positively hysterical. It seemed too absurd to talk of the weather; it was equally impossible to allude to the hopes and fears of impending matrimony. It was Lady Delachaine who broke the spell of silence.

"You have a nice face, my dear," she said meditatively, "though I don't altogether like the way you wear your hair. But I hope you are a Conservative?"

"I — I don't know," answered Bertha giddily. "I really am not quite sure—does it matter much?"

"Not very much," answered Lady Theo-
dosia shortly. "For of course, if you become
Lady Delachaine, you will have to be a
Conservative ; my brother is one."

This speech was calculated to rouse
Bertha's independent spirit ; she managed
to keep her temper, nevertheless, earnestly
wishing to do her best to create a good
impression on the minds of these future
relatives. She choked down both her
indignation and her desire to laugh.

"Politics are very engrossing to some
people," she said mildly.

Fortunately, at this juncture in the flag-
ging conversation, the door opened, and, to
Bertha's intense joy, Aggie appeared on
the scene.

The child came forward with her customary
look of extreme confidence in the gratification
of other people to receive her. This confidence was well founded, being generally

rewarded by success, for her face was so fair, her eyes so frank, and her general demeanour so engaging, together with her comical half-graceful, half-awkward movements—not unlike those of a young foal or an overgrown lamb—that it had seldom, if ever, been her fate to meet with a rebuff.

Yet, on this occasion, as she caught sight of the two strange figures, Aggie hesitated and paused midway in the room, gazing from one to the other of the visitors, as though seeking some encouragement to advance. Finally, her enquiring gaze rested upon Bertha; then, instinctively aware that her sister needed protection, she hurried forward, flung one arm round Bertha's neck, standing beside her, and pressing as closely as possible.

There was a moment's pause of stillness.

"You should shake hands, Aggie," then said the elder girl, looking tenderly up into her young champion's defiant eyes. "This is Lady Delachaine, and this Lady Theodosia. My little sister, Lady Delachaine — the dearest and best thing I have in the world."

"Till now," added Lady Theodosia sententiously.

"A very good girl, I am sure," said the old lady; "is her name Agnes or Agatha?"

"No; Julia," answered Bertha with haste, and feeling extremely guilty, she knew not why. "It is very foolish of me to call her Aggie, but somehow we always do it, don't we, Aggie?"

"Of course we do," was the sturdy reply.

"It seems odd," returned Lady Delachaine vaguely. Her eyes were wandering round the upper part of the room; she was considering whether such extraordinary windows were not liable to cause innumerable draughts.

" It sounds very odd indeed," said Lady Theodosia briskly. " Come here, my dear child, and tell me what you know."

Aggie moved half a step nearer to her questioner, but gave no answer.

" What do you do ? " continued Lady Theodosia. " Have you a governess ? "

" No," replied Aggie.

" Do you go to school ? "

" No," said Aggie.

" Dear, dear ! What would the school board say ! I suppose your sister teaches you ? The true gift of teaching is a very rare one ; don't you think so, Miss Millings?"

" Very," answered Bertha uncomfortably. She was, by this time, thoroughly frightened, for Aggie's accomplishments were peculiar though useful, and so unorthodox that she feared lest the child might be led on to recount them.

Certainly, her little sister was an adept in

the art of arranging and tidying a studio, cleaning brushes, setting a palette, and even laying in a rudimentary background if neces- sary. She was a first-rate (elementary) arithmetician, having been known to discover defects in the greengrocer's book that had eluded the vigilance of the rest of the house- hold. She had a pretty voice, though she was still so young, and could sing a few French ditties that Bertha had taught her, and also two or three German student-songs which Dr. Jackson had delighted to impart to her retentive ear. She possessed, as has already been said, shrewd common sense and mental capability much beyond her years, so tnat she was Bertha's counsellor as well as companion, and had seen and thought and even learned in a desultory way more than most children of her age. But of ordinary schoolroom education she was almost as ignorant as Jemima herself. If Aggie spoke

French and German with ease and fluency, it was because she and Bertha had spent a couple of winters abroad together; concerning the grammar and literature of either language, the little girl had never troubled herself, nor had any one troubled her.

Consequently, Bertha felt painfully that, in this asking of questions, Lady Theodosia pointedly alluded to the daily routine of a well-brought-up child. For the first time, perhaps, in her own life, the elder sister was disturbed by the reflection that her play-fellow knew but little of history or syntax, and was in outer darkness concerning the use of the globes.

"Aggie has been so much with me always," murmured Bertha apologetically.

"She must have masters," said Lady Theodosia, with off-hand cheeriness. "I can recommend several. I belong to a registry—also to a society for the special cultivation of the intellect of girls in their teens ; an admirable society. We meet once a fortnight."

" The poor little things have so much stuffed into their brains nowadays," said Lady Delachaine hesitatingly, " and of course you —she—her position will be very different."

Unconsciously, Lady Delachaine echoed Mrs. Weagles' prophecy. So thought Aggie, with a sinking heart.

" Perhaps the best, after all," said Lady Theodosia reflectively, " would be for the child to go to school."

But at this unwarrantable excess of inter-ference, Bertha fired up.

" Aggie will remain with me," she said.

" I shall learn what Bertha wishes," put in Aggie, drawing herself up with a defiant air, " and do what Bertha wants, and stay where Bertha likes."

" Oh, indeed ! " said Lady Theodosia

coldly. "And not listen to any one else's advice, I suppose?"

"Certainly not," retorted Aggie fiercely.

"A spoilt child," murmured Lady Theodosia with a sigh. "It is always a sad sight to see a spoilt child," she added, addressing Lady Delachaine.

"But Aggie is not spoilt!" cried Bertha, her voice trembling, partly from anger, partly in sorrowful astonishment. What? Did they think her own dear tender devoted little Aggie spoilt? She stretched out her arms to the child, who immediately nestled closely into them.

"Aggie never was spoilt," repeated Bertha, with great dignity.

But at this critical juncture, when the smouldering elements of opposition and dislike were about to leap into active flame, there came the sound of arrival at the door, which Jemima flung open with a sort of wide

consciousness of possessive grandeur, to
usher in the Earl of Delachaine, whose name
she had by this time thoroughly mastered.

Lord Delachaine stood for an instant at
the entrance of the studio, his quiet face
wearing an unaccustomed look of surprised
discomfort. But he readily grasped the
situation. He knew by the outline of Lady
Theodosia's back the exact frame of mind
she was in. His mother was never difficult
to read. As for Aggie—the centre of the
group—she had not chosen to take him into
her affections with the cordiality he deserved,
whilst he, on his side, could not quite forgive
the lukewarmness of her congratulations;
yet, even acknowledged neutrality between
him and Bertha's sister must verge into a
friendly alliance in the presence of sudden
difficulty and danger.

The earl advanced with a cordial manner.

"You here, mother?" he asked airily.

" And you, Dosia ? That's right—I am glad
to have met you on your first visit. Good
afternoon, Miss Julia ; I have just ordered
some flowers for you."

Then, moving towards Bertha, he took
her hand and bent over it, touching it lightly
with his lips, as he asked :

" What commands has the lady of my
heart to lay upon me ? "

At these words the two warriors of the
Delachaine family remained stonily rigid,
although the elder sighed audibly, whilst
tears came into Bertha's eyes, as, with both
hands, she almost clung to Lord Delachaine.
A sudden warmth of feeling, greater than
she had ever yet felt for him, rose ardently
within her. She had been so lonely before
his arrival! His action had been a graceful
one. There was indeed a natural charm
about him which advancing age had not
diminished, for grace of manner, like that of

thought, by no means belongs exclusively to the young.

Whilst his betrothed thus meditated in her gratitude, the earl gazed down at her with his most sphinx-like smile.

"I hope you have promised to come to us, Bertha," he said cheerfully. "It will be your turn now. Mother, have you asked her? And this little damsel also?"

"The house is yours, John," said Lady Theodosia with brevity, rising as she spoke.

"But my mother is its hostess," replied the earl.

"My dear John! my dear Dosia!" entreated Lady Delachaine nervously. Then, turning to Bertha, she faltered:

"Will you come Wednesday—the day after to-morrow?"

"The day after to-morrow, at luncheon—two o'clock," acquiesced the earl firmly; "and we will show you the family mansion. I am almost afraid you will call it a barrack. There is nothing picturesque about it. And ask Mary Baynham, Dosia; I have a sort of fancy that Bertha will get on with her. Now I will see you two to your carriage, and drive home with you if you like. My business is over for to-day."

Then, for all the ladies were too astonished to protest or even utter, the earl led the way out, still speaking as he went:

"Take care, here's a step, mother—let me give you an arm—that's the garden door, Dosia; please follow us."

And Lady Theodosia followed.

CHAPTER VIII.

THE Duchess of Baynham spent her life in a perpetual round of energetic pursuits. She managed to crowd into the available hours of each day as many fulfilled engagements as most of her friends completed in a week. At night she slept the peaceful sleep attributable to a good conscience and a good digestion, and awoke refreshed, and ready for the labours of the following day.

Young and pretty, she was moderately political, and ardently philanthropic, organizing, and conversational, whilst never too busy to do a kindness, even to a comparative stranger. It is not therefore surprising that she gathered around her a vast circle of acquaintance, amongst which were doubtless many satellites and some detractors and enemies, but also a fair sprinkling of really true and affectionate friends.

Continually occupied as she was, the duchess was enabled to make her triumphant way through multitudinous engagements only by means of the most carefully-regulated punctuality and method. She spent but a comparatively short time in the society of her husband, whose interests, being entirely sedentary and studious, lay in an opposite direction to her own. The duke was fond of solitude; the duchess was eminently gregarious and sociable. She wrote notes from early dawn to dewy eve; bought pamphlets on all sorts of humanitarian subjects, and glanced over and discussed the latest religious controversial works. Above all she belonged to and stoutly defended

from derision a curious group of friends—
men and women both—who termed themselves "the spirits," and who all were
pledged by solemn vows to study the same
difficult metaphysical books, and to meditate
on the same disquieting and unanswerable
questions.

The duke turned his back altogether upon
this and other bonds of society. He had
been engaged during the last twelve years
on a rhythmical translation of Dante, to
which should be appended copious notes and
explanations—a work which was to prove
superior to anything of the kind hitherto
attempted, and which must needs fill a want
long felt in the world of literature.

The duchess often bemoaned the seclusion
of her lord with a pretty bemoaning that
made some of her audience shrug their
shoulders, yet which possessed so undoubted
a ring of truth that many envied her husband.

even whilst blaming him for allowing her to go her own unfettered way rejoicing.

The Duchess of Baynham was first cousin to Lord Delachaine and Lady Theodosia. Her mother, sister to the late earl, had married Viscount St. Phippen, the possessor of much wealth and an exceedingly old title. It need scarce be chronicled here how the St. Phippens came over with the Conqueror, conscientiously bringing with them voluminous scrolls bearing the record of their genealogy for a tolerable number of previous centuries. Nor does any one doubt that the ruins of the Château de St. Fipin (sometimes in ancient archives spelt Phipin or Phipen) still stand—a pile of mournful grey stones — on the storm-tossed wave-bound shore of one of the most desolate points of Normandy.

It was now seven years since the only child and heiress of the English branch of the St. Phippens had been given in marriage to the present Duke of Baynham, then Lord Cassingdene, whose future estates were known to be heavily mortgaged, the property having become impoverished under the rule of his father and grandfather, two nobles of the good old reckless, hard-drinking, easy-living sort.   It had been agreed by the friends of both families that the union was in all respects an admirable one, and, when the two young people allowed themselves to be gently guided towards betrothal and marriage, nothing seemed wanting in the happy future before them.

Nor, since that brilliant wedding-day, had anything serious occurred to cause a change in public opinion; yet, especially during the first three or four years, the gossips of the town were not altogether satisfied.   The duke was seldom seen; the duchess, on the contrary, was too often seen.   So much

for their public life. As to their private
existence, the chief grievance was that no
one was admitted into it, whilst rumours
were afloat, rumours of hot and hasty words,
wrangles in fact—not to say quarrels. How
could it be otherwise ? The duchess was
evidently a headstrong woman ; so said the
duke's supporters. He was a selfish stay-at-
home misanthrope ; thus murmured the
partisans of the duchess.

Gradually, gossip died out — a painless
death—for want of natural sustenance, and
people turned readily to the far more
interesting scandals that were occurring
daily in other great families. The wedded
pair were let alone, to do as they pleased,
which indeed was a result they had long
desired, and whether they disagreed or dwelt
in peace became a matter of absolutely no
moment to anybody. Not even when Lord
Cassingdene succeeded to the dukedom, as

was the case shortly after his marriage, had
it been possible to glean any further details
of his character; nor, when his wife's parents
died, and her wealth was added to her
husband's income, did the busiest body record
any facts of real interest. They were evidently a commonplace couple.

Only, as need scarce be intimated, people
were always delighted to welcome the
duchess to their parties. On such occasions,
the host and hostess liked the sound of
her title, the men were one and all attracted
by her bright face and merry laugh, and,
strange to say, the women were seldom
jealous. "Perhaps because she is not
beautiful enough to cause envy," said one;
"perhaps because she mostly devotes herself
to some snuffy old person, whom nobody
talks to," said another.

The day after Bertha had received her
future relatives, the duchess was seated

according to custom at her writing-table, busily scribbling, when a footman entered, and presented to her a note from her cousin Theodosia. This was no unusual incident, as the two ladies, despite great differences of character, were on friendly and affectionate terms. On this special occasion, however, the duchess was much startled by the contents of the note, which, though it began with an invitation to lunch on the morrow, ended by a statement, curt and cold, of Lord Delachaine's engagement to Bertha Millings.

"There is no answer," said the duchess as quietly as she could. "Or rather, say I will go at once to Belgrave Square. And call me a hansom."

But left alone, being transfixed with astonishment, the recipient of the note gave vent to many exclamations. Good gracious! Mercy me! Who would have thought it! and so forth. Then, drawing a long breath, she jumped up from her seat, and proceeded hurriedly to tidy—some people might have said to untidy — her writing-table.

A gigantic and varied mass of papers was strewn upon this forbearing piece of furniture. Begging-letters, notices of committee-meetings, programmes of charity concerts, invitation cards and notes, and here and there lengthy and interesting epistles from some whose names stood high in the worlds of literature or science.

With difficulty, for her hands were positively trembling with eagerness, the duchess gathered up many of her papers in a chaotic bundle, and threw them into a drawer. Forthwith running upstairs—she mostly preferred to run than to walk—she donned her outdoor garments with the same vivacity that she brought to bear upon everything, and a few minutes later she was whirled off in her hansom.

On the way, however, she had thrust her head in at the secluded study, where the duke was, as usual, pacing up and down, his hands in the pockets of an old shooting-coat, his hair much ruffled, and his eyes fixed thoughtfully on the dingy ornamentation of the ceiling.

"You are going out?" he asked dreamily, as the door opened sufficiently to allow him to see the bonneted head of his wife nodding pleasantly at him.

"Just for an hour—only to Dosia's," she replied; "how are you getting on?"

"Pretty well," was the answer, with a long-drawn sigh. "I have not written much to-day. I was thinking over a most interesting treatise on the *terza rima*, sent to me by Professor Giovannini. You remember him at Pisa, don't you, Mary?"

"Oh yes, dear. He was a good-natured slow old thing, as tall and as crooked as the tower itself, with a beard a yard and a half long. And he was terribly fond of eating eggs at luncheon. Ah, those eggs! How little of them ever really reached his mouth!"

And the duchess, laughing, disappeared, closing the door gently.

Lady Theodosia was somewhat surprised when the answer to her note came in the shape of her cousin in person.

"I couldn't wait till to-morrow," began the eager visitor. "What, is it really, truly going to be? Had you any idea of it? To think of John, at last! John, caught, landed like other men! Let's sit down, Dosia, and you shall tell me all about it. It's too romantic—it really is! She's an artist, isn't she? And does she think of nothing but pictures?"

"Romantic, you call it?" echoed Lady
Theodosia with a bitter smile. "I call
it disgraceful, shameful." Thereupon she
launched forth into a lengthy and sour explanation of the terrible fate about to befal
the Delachaine family, owing to the projected
alliance with Miss Millings.

But when, at last, the angry narrator paused
to take breath her cousin, haply like Mother
Hubbard's dog, was actually laughing.

"After all, it might have been a great deal
worse, Dosia. Cheer up. Anyhow you and
I can't prevent it. If the girl is pretty and
ladylike—she is not of low origin, you say—
and if she is not vulgar and has no horrid
relations, I don't see that matters are quite
so bad as you make out. How dear old
John has managed to go free all these years,
I can't imagine! You should think of that!
And I should have hated a regular society
girl myself, or an American, even though it's

the thing, or an Australian! And it might have been an actress! Only think what stuck-up, worldly-wise creatures men often bring home to sit upon their simple-minded mothers and sisters! I do declare you ought to go down on your knees and be positively thankful."

"But, Mary, you don't realize it! Shall I describe our visit to you again?"

"No, no. It must have been horrid."

"It *was* horrid."

"For her too—poor little wretch! I wouldn't face you and Aunt Mary both together when you have, yes, just that expression in your eyebrows down to the corners of your mouth! I should have gone on the roof, or in the cellar!"

"Nonsense, Mary."

"I can't help it, Dosia. I think she must be a plucky girl to swallow the whole family."

"It is a pity she does swallow it, then. She does not appear very diffident."

"She is plucky, as I say. So is John, for that matter. Poor dear old John! Well, I shall be better able to console you to-morrow, Dosia. I shall have seen our new relative then. By-the-bye, what are we to call her?"

" Bertha," said Lady Theodosia, shortly.

"A good Anglo-saxon name. Perhaps her ancestors were yeomen, or squires— which is it? at the time of the Conquest. Do you think I might ask her? It would be so very interesting. I was skimming a most delightful paper the other day. It was read at the archæological meeting at Newington-cum-ditchpool by the great Midgkins—you know who I mean—who sent it me, only I've forgotten most of it. But it said—oh yes, I remember—the archers in olden days didn't care to make bows out of English yew-trees—it was the Spanish yews that were so highly thought of."

"Indeed," said Lady Theodosia calmly. She was used to her cousin's divagations, and seldom followed or interrupted them.

"It is so difficult to keep up with everything," continued the duchess, sighing. "Oh! and Dosia! What *do* you say to this?"

The speaker jumped up, and pointed triumphantly to her own left shoulder whereon, amidst folds of soft lace and bead trimmings, reposed two badges: the first, an enamel brooch representing a primrose, the second a simple knot of dark blue ribbon.

"Of course, Dosia, you know I have a habitation to look after; but I hadn't told you about the other, eh? I signed the pledge only yesterday. It's an excellent thing to do nowadays."

"I've no doubt of it," said Lady Theodosia,

frigidly. " I belong to five total abstinence societies and the Church Temperance one myself, though I do not wear any decorations."

" But the blue ribbon's half the battle, don't you think so ? Force of example and all that. The only drawback is that at the boat-race people are sure to think I'm all for Oxford, whereas Cas swears by Cambridge —was brought up there, you know—that's to say there and Eton—and they're both light blue—really, Dosia, I quite wish you were a comfortable drunkard! It would have been such fun to convert you !"

"Thank you," said Lady Theodosia drily.

"And how about the pretty artist ? Painters are given to drinking, I believe. Isn't there a proverb ?"

"No, that has to do with fiddlers," said Lady Theodosia, who this time relaxed into a smile.

"Or lords," continued the duchess imper-

turbably.   "'Drunk as a fiddler, drunk as
a lord.'   I wonder why?   It is a very
curious question ; don't you think so, Dosia ?
I'll write by this afternoon's post to Dr.
Monkshood.   He has written the most
beautifully-convincing paper on legal techni-
calities in Patagonia.   He's perfectly sure to
know about proverbs.   And now tell me
something else."

The duchess was standing in front of the
fireplace, gazing at her own reflection in the
looking-glass, and patting the sides of her
bonnet with her two little soft gloved hands.

"Don't you think this is quite the dearest
darlingest bonnet you ever saw, Dosia ?   I
walked down Regent Street the other day
and looked in at all the shop-windows—it
was great fun—and I finally invested in this
bonnet.   It's what my little friend the
Marquise de Grosgrain would call 'tout ce
qu'il y a de plus fin de siècle.'"

"I do wish," protested Lady Theodosia severely, "I do really wish, Mary, that you would give up seeing quite so much of that silly Frenchwoman."

"My dear girl, she is quite the 'haute volée,' I assure you. Cas says her husband is cocksure—that's not *my* word, so don't shake your head again—cocksure of being ambassador somewhere or other next time there's a change. Besides, her mother was a Croque-mitaine, and that means a great deal in itself, you know. But now I really must be off. I've got a meeting of the Friendly girls at half-past twelve, and some sewing mothers to look up after that, and poor old Cas is always so lonely if I'm not in to lunch. I really scarcely ever see him now. Good-bye, dear, or rather 'sans adieu.' Two o'clock to-morrow. I'm *so* curious to see the little painter, you can't think! Don't you be downhearted, Dosia. Marriage is a lottery,

and women are to men just what men think
them.   Suppose you and I had found a real
paragon, do you imagine that John would
have cared about her?   He, as your brother,
was bound to fish somebody out for himself
whom you would detest.   That is, at first.
Try to like her, Dosia dear, if only for your
own sake."

"For my own sake?" repeated Lady
Theodosia proudly.

"Well, yes, just a little.   If John is really
fond of her, you oughtn't to make it too
miserable for him.   He'll only like her the
better."

"And me the less!   Thank you, Mary."

"I did not quite say that.   Try for John's
sake, then."

"Ah, for John's sake!"

"He may not be as altogether happy as
you think."

"He is at any rate happy enough about
her."

" Well, is not that as it should be ? "

" If only it had been some one else ! "

" Yes, I know ; Lady Cecilia. Well, I will promise to criticize severely to-morrow. Poor John ! Poor old John ! Good-bye again, Dosia ! No, never mind ringing. I'm awfully late ! Poor old John ! Good-bye, good-bye ! "

CHAPTER IX.

IT was three minutes before two o'clock on the following day, when Bertha and Aggie stood beneath the ugly portico which enabled Lord Delachaine's mansion so closely to resemble its neighbours. The sisters had elected to seek their destination on foot, having pronounced themselves ready to start so early that their chief danger lay in arriving too soon.

Aggie had carefully superintended Bertha's toilet, and Bertha had equally tenderly arrayed her little sister. Aggie put a good face on the whole matter, for she could see that her darling's spirits were drooping and perturbed. Only once, when Jemima had come into the room, and Bertha had gone out of it for a moment, did the child give vent to her genuine feelings.

"It's just like going to the dentist, Jemima!" she exclaimed sorrowfully.

"Laws, miss!" replied that confidant soothingly, and with real charity considering that her mouth was full of pins. "Don't you go for to worrit yourself, there's a lamb. They ought to be proud to have two such pretty faces as Miss Bertha's and yours a-coming into the family, which it seems terrible sparing of good looks. Though beauty's naught but a fleeting show," added Jemima, suddenly remembering her favourite tenets.

Now, at last, the destination had been reached, neither too soon, nor yet too late.

"Isn't it fishes?" asked Aggie suddenly, and enigmatically.

"Fishes, dear?" repeated Bertha, surprised.

"Fishes and serpents and frogs, I mean, who've got cold blood."

"Why, dear, why?"

"Nothing, Booffles; I suppose they get along just as well as other creatures, don't they? Oh! do you know I could really begin to wish we hadn't had to come. They're going to open the door!"

"Of course they are," said Bertha with dignity. Then, almost unnecessarily giving her name, she and her sister followed the butler upstairs. Winslow, to whom the reader has already been introduced, was an old family servant, and as such cast many furtive glances in Bertha's direction—glances prompted not by curiosity alone, but also by interest in the family, and even by hopefulness for the future.

"My word! There will be changes!" thought Winslow to himself, as he viewed the bright young faces; but aloud he merely politely offered to relieve Bertha from the weight of her umbrella! Then, in a triumphant voice, he heralded the arrival of " Miss Millings and Miss Julia Millings."

Whilst Aggie scarcely recognized her own identity under this imposing name, the occupants of the drawing-room seemed for the nonce equally disconcerted, although, naturally, the visitors had been expected.

The room was large, opening with folding doors into another apartment, that was smaller but equally cheerless. Both had been evidently decorated some fifty years ago, when solid walnut furniture, elaborate gilt cornices, velvet pile carpets strewn with giant roses, and white and gold papering, were just coming into vogue. A ceiling, rich with mouldings of no particular style or design, loomed heavily above the naked walls, whose lofty bareness was sparsely broken, yet not relieved, by two or three large mirrors.

Round the rooms were ranged some marble-topped consoles, whereon a few empty *jardinières* and other pieces of Sèvres china were the only ornaments. Meanwhile, the armchairs and ottomans, covered with shiny old-fashioned chintz, were placed at such decorous intervals round the polished centre table that they seemed no more intended for use than the table itself, which was scattered over with stray books, methodically piled, and tall glasses supporting lanky grass, immortelles, and dried bulrushes.

Perhaps, after all, Lady Theodosia's davenport and high stool, and cumbrous basket of poor people's clothes in process of making, all crowded together in what was known as " Dosia's corner," gave their only life-like appearance to the dreary rooms.

The Delachaine family were on the present occasion grouped in a sort of chilly settlement of bleached chintz furniture, ostentatiously waiting. The daughter of the house sat upright on a loosely-shrouded chair of nondescript form. Her mother leaned back amongst many slippery cushions at the end of a large sofa, beside which same end Lord Delachaine was standing very upright and expectant, whilst on the other the duchess had gracefully balanced herself, her tiny feet (encased in the smartest and shiniest of boots) dangling, and her gloved hands rattling their many bangles and gesticulating at every remark made by their owner.

When the new-comers entered, Lady Delachaine rose as hastily as she was able, and advanced to greet them, followed by her son who, to Bertha's eyes, had an unfamiliar brushed-up appearance, which made her instantaneously shy and silent. The earl was at all times irreproachably neat and tidy; but to-day there was surely an air of constraint about the cut of his coat and the

turn of his necktie. The same stiff politeness pervaded Lady Delachaine's black silk,
whilst from every seam of Lady Theodosia's
tight tweed costume peeped an angry though
suppressed superciliousness.

Bertha's depression was doubtless infec-
tious, as Aggie had caught it already; even
the earl seemed speedily to participate in it.
Under these novel circumstances, he appeared
scarce happier than his guests, yet his voice
was cordial as ever when he greeted his
betrothed, and there was even the faint ghost
of a smile visible on one side of his grave
mouth.

"Dear, dear!" began Lady Delachaine,
who was at a loss what to say, after the first
formal greeting. But the duchess, who had
alighted gently on the points of her toes,
came swiftly to the rescue.

"Introduce me at once, John!" she exclaimed. "This is Miss Millings, isn't it?

I must call you Bertha at once. You look
so like a Bertha, with such nice soft golden
hair. Will you give me a kiss? And this
is your little sister of whom Dosia told me
so much ?"

Here Lady Theodosia glanced reprovingly
at her cousin, but the latter, mentally gliding
from what she would herself have termed
an unavoidable tarradiddle, proceeded gaily :

"Do let's all sit down on this big sofa.
Now, Bertha, you absolutely *must* take your
cloak off! Dosia, my dear, how abominably
your poor people's things smell of flannel!
Don't you always wonder, Bertha—I must
call you Bertha, you know—why poor people's
things so persistently smell of flannel ?

"Things that are made of flannel smell
of flannel," said Lady Theodosia severely.

Bertha could not help laughing, neither
could the earl. Lady Delachaine, looking
almost pleased, gave the offending basket a

slight push with her thin old hand. Only
Lady Theodosia remained grave, but the
slight push sent the basket reeling against
the table—some flannels fell out and seemed
to set all the ornaments in tremulous motion.
One of the tall glasses wavered for a moment,
then slowly capsized, happily to be caught in
Lord Delachaine's outstretched arms, whilst
a very cascade of novels tumbled to the floor.

Aggie jumped forward to pick up the
volumes ; so did Bertha ; so did the duchess,
whose head came in such close proximity to
Aggie's that the two were nearly knocked
together, at which the duchess laughed, and
Aggie smiled, though in a frightened way.
Like a jarring note came the incisive tones
of Lady Theodosia's voice.

"That's the best part of those dry bulrushes," she remarked ; "they require no
water."

"So I should imagine," said the earl.

The duchess went into another unreasoning fit of laughter.

"What a funny girl you are, Dosia!" she exclaimed after a little spasmodic paroxysm; and Bertha, who in her wildest moments could not have alluded to Lady Theodosia as a funny girl, admired the courage of the duchess exceedingly.

"Why, here's the very book," exclaimed that voluble lady, "the very thing I've been hunting out for days at all the libraries!"

"What is it?" asked Lord Delachaine, with as much show of interest as he could muster.

"It's a novel written by a man," replied his cousin. "That's why all the ladies want to read it. Don't you know, John, that when a man does condescend to write a naughty book he piles and ladles it on, whilst poor women—though they're always getting unjustly abused—only dare to deal out bad things, in tea-spoonfuls, or tiny, tiny pills and powders—homeopathically, so to speak."

The earl looked pained.

"How you do run on, Mary. Besides, I am not quite sure of the facts of the case."

"My dear child!" expostulated Lady Delachaine.

"What will Miss Millings think of you, Mary?" asked Lady Theodosia sourly.

The duchess put on a look of the blandest innocence, but even this did not soften the heart of the earl.

"Your one weakness, Mary," he said in a low tone, "is to make us all think you as bad as possible, whereas——"

"Whereas?" asked the culprit defiantly.

Her laughing brown eyes suddenly met Aggie's. The child was standing scarce a yard in front, staring with all her might. In vain did Bertha give a gentle pull at her little sister's sash—Aggie stared on.

The duchess did not object; there was something in that childish face which had taken her fancy from the very first. She had intended to like Bertha, and to make great friends with her, but, as the two visitors entered, she had quickly turned aside from the elder sister to watch the younger. With the close consideration which she brought to bear on most things, despite her carelessness of speech, the duchess was accustomed to watch and take note of all around her.

"Whereas?" she repeated enquiringly; "you shall give the verdict, little Julia. Do you think I am bad?"

Aggie, whose eyes had never wavered from the countenance of the duchess, whose liking she already returned—for surely magnetic attraction is usually as reciprocal as it is instantaneous—Aggie hesitated, but only for a moment. There was just one instant of awful silence which terrified Bertha, so that she reddened and grew hot; then Aggie advanced a step, and with her sweet mouth broadening into a very genuine smile, that was no longer affected by shyness or nervousness :

" I think you are very good," she said.

The duchess stretched out her arms, and in her impulsive way drew Aggie close, and covered her face with kisses.

"You are a dear little thing!" she exclaimed. "Will you be my friend? Now, John, you see," she added, looking triumphantly up at the earl, " everybody doesn't judge me as you do."

" I only spoke of how you meant us to judge you," he answered quietly.

But there was no further discussion, for luncheon was announced. Lady Delachaine invited Bertha to accompany her downstairs, and the whole party adjourned to the dining-room.

CHAPTER X.

A FEW weeks passed. To Bertha her present
life seemed like one of those pleasant dreams
which sometimes occur when, conscious that
we are half asleep, we are unwilling to wake.
The change and excitement that came with
every rising sun, the numberless trifling
engagements of each morning and each
afternoon, prevented her from sitting down to
think. The immediate present was certainly
delightful; the future, if considered at all,
appeared fair and easy. Bertha was floating
down a smooth and shining river; the earl
was steering, and with his strong and skilful
arm warding her from rocks or other perils.
She could see nothing before her but a

prosperous sunlit view. Her old studio life seemed already years behind. Her betrothed, with his kindly grave courtesy, and delicate attentiveness, was surely more suited to her than a younger and less polished lover might have been ; and his position (with the agreeable expect-ancy of her own), his sheltering care, his wealth even—all brought within her capacity many unforeseen advantages and pleasures that were to her an almost tangible happiness.

One day came a gracious letter from Lady Delachaine, enclosing a cheque for two hundred pounds, which she begged Bertha to accept as a help towards the necessary trousseau. Miss Millings' pride was up in arms for a moment, but was soon stilled again by the benevolent terms in which the letter was couched. Moreover, it was certainly pleasant to be treated with deference

in shops, where her engagement became
speedily known, for, though Bertha was by
no means vulgar, her path had not always
been strewn with such thornless roses as now
fell to her lot, and during the six and twenty
years of her life she had known many
struggles and privations; possibly, indeed,
Aggie herself had scarcely been aware of
them all.

Meanwhile, to Aggie, the passing days
shewed only the reverse of the gilded medal.
She would not allow herself to lament old
times, yet, occasionally, she longed to throw
her arms round the dusty easels, and caress
them like friends—silent friends who had
shared happy bygone hours with her, and
who were now obliged to learn the hard
lesson of neglect. Aggie herself was not
precisely neglected; that could not be
admitted. Bertha's love for her was as
strong as ever, and, if Lord Delachaine's

betrothed felt in honour bound to consider him before any other person, her feelings towards Aggie had not necessarily undergone any change. Bertha walked or drove with her elderly lover every day; she went with him to choose a horse, a pony-carriage, a necklace and other items; she often dined or lunched at the family mansion, which, to do her justice, she had never yet viewed with envy. There were a fairly numerous number of Delachaine relations to whom, of course, it was necessary that the future countess should be introduced. Sometimes, when she appeared, her little sister accompanied her, but, though a few people talked to the child, and apparently endeavoured to put her at her ease, Aggie—who was odd in some things—shewed no partiality for the new society into which she found herself suddenly thrown. She infinitely preferred remaining at home with Jemima, or spending a couple of quiet hours with old Mrs. Weagles.

Bertha who, consequently, went forth often alone, made some way with her future relations, though Lady Theodosia remained frigid and disagreeable, whilst Lady Dela-chaine was so mentally limp as to be practically useless as a defender. The duchess was invariably friendly, though in truth her heart went out chiefly to Aggie, and the latter returned this affection with an ardour that was all the more conspicuous from her general coldness. Moreover, when the two Miss Millings were invited to the ducal abode, Aggie pleased not only the duchess, but the duke exceedingly. As his lively spouse afterwards remarked, she had never before seen him so taken with anybody but a learned professor, whilst of himself she enquired :

" Dear Cas, isn't it a dreadful pity that my

cousin John didn't wait a bit longer, so as to marry that dear little person instead of her sister ?   Not that I don't like Bertha, and of course he would have been as old as the hills, but he's old now, there's no use denying it, and really he's waited so long already—— "

" He might have waited a little *too* long," replied the duke grimly, turning over the worn pages of his Dante.

About this time a great discontent fell upon Aggie's mind regarding herself.   She fought hard to be unselfish, and she blamed herself exceedingly for not entering more fully into Bertha's happiness.   This betrothal was the first thing that had in any way appeared to divide the sisters, and, however earnestly they mutually strove against the patent fact, it was evident to both of them that they had become a little—just a very little—not estranged, but divided.   For the first time in her life the elder sister did not

shew every one of her letters to the younger,
whilst there often arrived a particularly aggres-
sive square envelope, bearing a small coronet
and initial, that Aggie learned to know well,
and equally to detest. The very aspect of
it was annoying, with its "Miss Millings"
written in small precise caligraphy, and the
D. down in the left-hand corner according
to old-fashioned custom, though it was surely
unnecessary further to advertize the writer
of that ever-recurring epistle.

Sometimes, as she lay awake at night,
Aggie would make new resolutions to throw
off the growing constraint she felt in con-
versing with her sister of Lord Delachaine,
and to put on with her morning garments
the very brightest and most joyous smile
which she could possibly assume. But the
light of day brings many of our good resolutions to naught, and Aggie acknowledged to
herself, with regret, how repeatedly she failed.

Once she appealed to Jemima. Lady Theodosia's words deeply rankled in the child's heart, and she often wondered whether in truth she had been hopelessly spoilt.

" Do *you* think I am spoilt, Jemima ? " she asked one day.

" Lawk-a-mussy, little miss ! " was the astonished answer. " It's some of us as is spoilt, that's positive. But to my thinking 'taint you. All our hearts is black—as black as black, and that's the fact of it, and them that's whitest often turns out to be the black ones after all."

With which doubtful consolation Aggie was fain to be content.

The wedding-day was now fixed ; it was to be in the last week of April. Indeed there was no reason for delay. The generous settlements made by Lord Delachaine were of so simple a description as not to detain the most dilatory of lawyers. Bertha, needless to say, had no legal arrangements to make. Her future husband was undesirous of overstepping his next birthday; Lady Theodosia had already uttered every unpleasant remark which could be made on the subject of the marriage; Bertha was docile, Aggie silent, as to dates and arrangements. There was no one else to consult.

Meanwhile, though Miss Millings had no relations, she had more friends than she seemed to have counted upon, for, when her fortunate engagement was made known, numbers of people flocked to visit and congratulate her. They one and all agreed in their approval of the marriage. It was *so* delightful, *so* charming, *so* satisfactory in every way. The artists of her acquaintance held Bertha to be a lucky girl, and spoke kindly on the subject, but did not trouble her about this time. Assuredly, they were greatly occupied with their pictures for the various spring exhibitions, and the attending anxiety of such work, after which, as every one knows, they would hate the very mention of paint and painting, and would be tempted to shun each other's studios for a while.

There was, however, one of these friends whom Bertha sometimes regretted that she could not go to see. He was an old and tried friend—Henry Eldon by name—and likewise a man of acknowledged genius : but, in this present dream-life of hers, whatever her good intentions might be, the right moment never came for carrying them out. Eldon lived some little way out of town; he was not fond of interruptions; he had not written any congratulatory letter; it was even rumoured that he had gone off on a sketching trip—all these were good and weighty reasons. On the other hand, and despite narcotics, Bertha's conscience occasionally

awoke to whisper that she owed Eldon
the debt of an ancient and true friendship,
and that, in former days, when she had
needed encouragement, and even valuable
recommendations and introductions, Eldon
had never pleaded business nor insufficiency
of time or inclination.

Oddly enough, and perhaps by force of
contrast, it was during a prolonged interview
with her dressmaker one day that Bertha's
mind recurred persistently to the bygone
times when, to her great joy, she had been
allowed to wield a brush in a corner of the
great painter's studio, when her one ambition,
the one idea that filled and almost over-
flowed her soul, was a life dedicated to the
art which she firmly believed she loved, a
life gladly given up to that glorious calling of
which she was but an humble votary, whilst
he, Eldon, was past master, standing in his
old age even higher on the ladder of fame

than he had stood in the strength and prime
of manhood.

Was it a presentiment which on this
afternoon made Bertha quicken her steps till
she reached her own door, and then receive
without surprise Jemima's intimation that
Mr. Eldon was waiting in the studio?

As Bertha ran into the room without
a moment's delay, her face aglow with
pleasure, her hands stretched out in greeting,
a slight bent figure rose from the depths of
an armchair.

" It is I, Miss Millings, "said a voice that
was as mellow as the tones of a violoncello;
" I hope this pleasant welcome is really
meant for me. Did you know that I took
your hospitality for granted?"

" Oh Mr. Eldon!" exclaimed Bertha; " I
am so glad to see you!   Why, it is a perfect
age since we have met!"

" Yes, it is an age," replied the visitor,

who, having resumed his comfortable chair, sat thoughtfully stroking his grey beard. " I don't know that it is altogether my fault. I am not good at making calls. You know that, my dear child. In the old days, it was you who used to come and look me up from time to time."

"I have been very busy," said Bertha apologetically.

"Yes, yes, I know, of course. Do you think I am such a crabbed old Diogenes as not to understand? Only I want you to know that I have been busy too ; perhaps not quite so pleasantly," added the old man with a smile.

" Oh, Mr. Eldon ! "

"Well, to-night I have taken you by storm, haven't I ? Jemima told me that you were gone out in one direction, and Julia in another. But she said encouragingly: ' If you like to go and make yourself comfortable

in the studio, sir, and wait a bit, why, maybe
as maybe Miss Bertha won't be long.' She
even went so far as to offer me some refresh-
ment. 'Painting's hard work, ain't it, sir?'
she said. She knows I am an artist, you
see—— "

"Why, of course she knows it," said
Bertha, smiling.

"I shall be quite proud of my fame,
henceforth," said Eldon.

"It was quite right of Jemima to offer
you tea. I was very remiss."

"No, no—I don't want any. It is I who
am remiss in not wishing you joy. My
dear child "—here the painter rose and took
both Bertha's hands gently in his—" look
me straight in the face and tell me : are you
really happy? I am more than old enough
to be your father, you see, and I have known
you since you were so high. Why, it was
owing to my advice that you took your first

steps on the steep hillside of Parnassus ; wasn't it ? "

" I am a backslider on that slippery incline," interposed Bertha, laughing confusedly.

" Never mind about art," quoth the artist. " What I want to know is if you are happy. I do most truly hope it; I want you to be happier than anybody ever was before."

Bertha felt slightly uncomfortable beneath those clear questioning eyes.

" Oh, Lord Delachaine is so kind," she answered at last. " I am sure I have done right."

" That is what I wanted to be certain of," said the other, releasing her hands, and returning to his chair, whilst an expression of satisfaction passed across his fine face. " You know I have never been married myself, and it has always seemed to me that there must come a moment, even in the midst of content like yours, when the fortunate human being must needs sit down face to face with all its old doubts and fears, to ask itself tremblingly : What have I done ? What *have* I done ? Is this for the best, or is it not ? "

" It doesn't do," said Bertha stoutly, " it doesn't do, really, to analyze things too closely, Mr. Eldon."

" No, perhaps not," replied her friend musingly ; " only to some natures it is almost impossible not to doubt when standing on the brink—— "

" Don't, Mr. Eldon ! " said Bertha with a little laugh. " Would you have me believe that marriage is the brink of a horrible precipice ? We women, you know, are always taught from our earliest infancy that a wedding is the highest goal we can look forward to."

" True," answered her companion, " and

I did not mean anything so dreadful as my words seem to have implied. Nay, my dear girl, without arguing on woman's rights or wrongs, nor on man's either for that matter, a really happy marriage must be the perfection of everything here on earth. If only it were not almost too difficult of attainment to us mortals, too bright a thing, like the sun, for our weak vision to contemplate. ' Glissez mortels, n'appuyez pas,' is an axiom perhaps specially intended for married couples."

" It is a question of give and take," said Bertha sedately.

Eldon turned to look at her. Was she really happy? He wondered again, but he did not ask.

The light was shining full on his head. What a fine face it was, with its rugged brow, seamed with lines which told of many a hard fight fought out in solitude between high aims and unexpected shortcomings of achievement—a soldier's scars won in dark hours of difficulty and depression.

"Nay, I hope that you are at the gate of an earthly paradise; that is what I meant to say," said the artist at last, speaking with an unexplained change of voice. "Why, I have known you, Bertha, since you were five years old! So I may wish you good luck now and always; and may you be happy!"

Eldon left his seat as he spoke, and walked quickly across to one of the easels on which stood an unfinished picture.

"And so all this is to be done away with," he said with a sudden laugh that sounded almost harsh. "Art is to be like an old neglected sultana, poked in a bag with a big stone, and dropped away into the sea in the middle of the night of forgetfulness. Is it not so?"

"Oh, I hope not!" said Bertha eagerly.

"Lord Delachaine has promised me a charming studio. He says there is a tower at Delachaine Court, which I can make into a regular painting-room."

"Yes, yes, I know," returned Mr. Eldon morosely. " You will go into the room once every three weeks and find it cold and cheerless, and your colours quite dry, and you will heave a little sigh of regret and go downstairs, and put on a fine frock, and drive out in a coach and four."

" I hope not necessarily a coach and four!" said Bertha, laughing.

" Why not ?" asked Eldon gruffly. " Ah, my dear, plenty of fine things have been said by wiser folks than I to prove that Art is a jealous mistress—in a lady's case perhaps I should say a jealous tyrant—who will brook no rival, no equal."

Bertha remained silent. Then her friend, bending to take up a small picture which he had previously placed out of sight, offered it to her as he said :

" I have brought you a present, to make my tardy good wishes the more acceptable. Will you take it ? It is the little head I was once allowed to paint from yourself. Possibly, the rival I was mentioning just now might care for it."

Bertha was effusive in her thanks, though the tone of the giver was still somewhat jarring.

"Ah !" she went on to say, holding the canvas up to the light, "ah, if I only looked like that, how delightful it would be ! You don't flatter in your words, Mr. Eldon, but you do with your brush, I fear."

" No, no !" cried the artist aggrieved ; "is it possible to flatter nature ? Come, child, you are enough of an artist yourself to know that, whatever we may do, we cannot give life and animation, the changing carnations of the cheek, and the liquid brightness of the eyes, as we would wish. Even if you were not what you are—but what is the use of talking? You understand me well enough."

"I think I know what you mean," rejoined Bertha hurriedly; "but I know also that we see the worst of our own selves, and think the very worst too."

Eldon began to pace up and down the room.

"It is a curious thing," he said, "that we all wish ourselves physically different. Possibly, I should like to be a big burly fellow, whilst you surely desire to have ink-black hair and almond-shaped eyes. *Chi lo sa?* Whereas, regarding inward grace, we are generally pretty well satisfied in the main. If we have a fault or two, we are very lenient on the subject. If we are extra proud, we say: *that* is a good kind of fault after all. If we are spendthrifts, we call ourselves generous; stingy, we consider ourselves thrifty. We seldom, if ever, consider our bad qualities to be really bad. Now, is not this a strong proof that we care less about our real natures than about our outside looks? What do you think?"

But, before Bertha had time to give her opinion on this knotty point, the door opened, and Lord Delachaine appeared.

He was delighted to make acquaintance with the celebrated Mr. Eldon, who, on his part, was much taken by the earl's stately courtesy, his evident interest in serious things, and his affection for Bertha—which latter sentiment must indeed have been patent to a far less keen observer than the painter.

The two men were a great contrast: Lord Delachaine, tall, erect, especially English-looking, and high-born but unpoetic in appearance. Eldon, with something in his rugged picturesque countenance that recalled Albert Dürer's knight, as well as a southern ease and suppleness of figure, and warmth and excitability of expression—for his grandmother had been an Italian. Meanwhile, between them was Bertha, sunny-haired and smiling, sitting, as it were, betwixt the spirit of her artist's craft and the promise of her woman's happiness.

For Eldon was there to-day like a spirit indeed of something that is dying—fleeting, if not yet quite dead. When, presently, he took his leave, Bertha heaved a long sigh. He had brought a vibration almost of pain into this new and brilliant life of hers.

And, whilst Lord Delachaine, in his meditative way, was saying :

"Capital fellow, that! I like him, Bertha. Those great men, when you do come to know them, certainly have a charm——"

his betrothed was hastily hiding away with its face to the wall the sketch that was, as she thought (and despite Lord Delachaine's opinion) an image far prettier than the real Bertha Millings, who had been oh! so light-hearted, and yet so curiously serious-minded, in those bygone working days.

There is a familiar French saying : " Ah, le bon vieux temps quand j'étais si malheureux!" We are all of us prone to ponder and sigh in this vein sometimes. But Bertha was not mourning over the past now. Far from it. She turned to Lord Delachaine with a face as placid as a summer sea. If a vestige of doubt had arisen in her mind, it had been speedily and successfully banished from thence.

CHAPTER XI.

AGGIE's friend Mrs. Weagles, who lived next door, had for the last two years been deeply interested in the doings of her young neighbours. Indeed, it may be said that Mrs. Weagles was interested in all her neighbours, the apparent object of her life being to gratify her inveterate love of gossip, which was based on a most untiring and irrepressible curiosity. This was a fault, doubtless, but a kindly one, as the old lady bubbled over with sympathy for the whole human race, and most especially for that portion of it which dwelt in her own street. She was never ill-natured, so that, after all, what could it matter that she benevolently discussed everybody's past, present, and future, and wanted to know a great deal more about them than they knew themselves?

Her house, though exceedingly small, offered unusual advantages to a person of her enquiring nature. A bay-window in the little front sitting-room where she usually sat commanded the street, whilst her bedroom at the back judiciously overlooked, not only her own narrow strip of garden, but the similar strips on either side, Bertha's somewhat larger territory included.

Mrs. Weagles had from the first formed an attachment to Aggie, which was strange, considering that the child was unusually reticent, and owned but few tastes in common with her new friend. However, people are not always as consistent as we expect them to be, and certain it is that the yellow old fingers would eagerly tap at the window, and beckon to the little next-door neighbour whenever there was the least opportunity or encouragement for so doing.

Mrs. Weagles was small of figure, bent, and partly paralyzed, and clad habitually in black garments of no particular shape or fashion. On Sundays and holydays, however, or when she was specially arrayed for visitors, she wore a cap trimmed with copious loops of mauve ribbon, and a comfortable white shetland shawl that enveloped her almost entirely, and from which her hands, emerging with pleasant idleness to lie folded on her lap, in themselves suggested gentle gossip and friendly enquiry.

On many an afternoon she sat thus, robed in her best, and ensconced in her large arm-chair by the bay-window. To facilitate her investigations, a couple of small looking-glasses had been cunningly arranged in order to reflect the passers-by, as well as those who mounted the steps of her own

door, and these mirrors (it must be owned),
despite Aggie's lack of general curiosity,
were always a source of much amusement to
that young person. One of them was convex,
and therein the moving picture was delight-
fully diminutive ; cabs, carts, and people
grew or dwindled, but never appeared much
larger than tiny toys, whilst even the dull
street and grimy houses seemed attractive by
reason of the liliputian scale of reproduction.
If, by happy chance, the sky was blue, or
flecked with fleecy clouds, the picture was all
the prettier, thought Aggie.

On one agreeable afternoon, Mrs. Weagles
was too excited to sit as placidly as usual.
With the forefinger of her right hand gently
tapping the outstretched palm of her left, she
was carefully counting and enumerating.

"I think I have got them right!" she
exclaimed triumphantly. "First, the brown
morning dress, then the rich velvet for

luncheon wear, the dark blue satin robe for afternoon visiting—also, yes, I musn't forget the striped black and white afternoon. Isn't it striped, dear?"

"Yes," said Aggie, nodding her head.

"Now," continued Mrs. Weagles, cautiously treading amongst the perils of word-painting, "now, I think, my love, I am not wrong—there is a pink and white tea-gown, embroidered with white silk, as well as the pale blue one."

Aggie acquiesced again. She was busy with a chaotic mass of knitting wherein she was trying to discover and pick up Mrs. Weagles' dropped stitches.

"Of course," continued that lady loftily, "I can't count in the wedding-dress. That goes *song deer*, as people say ; but I don't feel quite certain about the evening gowns. Did you tell me there was a brown satin ? I think it sounds a trifle old for your dear sister."

"Yes," said Aggie ; "a brown satin trimmed with Venetian point."

" Ah !" said Mrs. Weagles, drawing a long breath and metaphorically smacking her lips. " Venetian point, I think you said, dear, that the Duchess of Baynham has given as a present ? And a white china crêpe, and a cool heliotrope silk besides ? Dear, dear !"

But, in the very midst of this splendid catalogue, the enumerator's attention was suddenly diverted.

"Goodness gracious !" she exclaimed, peering earnestly into one of the looking-glasses. " If that isn't Lena Walters strutting up and down the street with Richard Vaughan ! I do wonder if there's anything up, I do really. And there, on old Miss Wedmore's doorstep, I see her maid Drusilla. Julia, my love, quick, go and call my Susan ! Tell her to step over and speak to Drusilla —no, tell her to come here and speak to me

instead; I really must know all about it.
Why! How those two are going on, to be
sure, prancing and talking, and bowing and
smiling! And Drusilla looking after them
as sharp as sharp; I'll be bound she knows
more than we any of us do, for all she
looks so prim! And they say that Miss
Wedmore doesn't like her to be gossip-
ing about with the other servants—but
my Susan's so different! Besides, she can
just step across and ask how Miss Wedmore's wrist is getting on. I hear she
sprained it quite badly last week opening
the window; those new-fangled windows
are so heavy, what with fancy panes and
lead lines! My love, do call Susan; quick,
there's a dear!"

"Won't it do another time, dear Mrs.
Weagles?" asked Aggie imploringly; "please
let me tell you some more about Bertha's
gowns now."

"Well, dear," replied Mrs. Weagles good-naturedly; "so you shall if you like. Of course I was anxious to know about those two young things, for people say Mr. Vaughan's a most excellent young man, and his father is really well off—everything so comfortable, you know! Still, your sister's beautiful dresses interest me very much. You haven't told me about the 'going away' costume."

"No," said Aggie, a little sadly. She was not fond of realizing that Bertha must go away, even though she were to be robed in the most elegant and perfect of costumes.

"It's grey," she said gently.

"Grey!" repeated Mrs. Weagles; "well now, that *is* exciting! For there's grey and grey, you know, my love—all sorts of grey. Is it French grey, or pearl grey, or silver grey, or lavender grey?"

"A very pretty shade," replied Aggie carelessly; then, somewhat contrite, she added:

"The beautifullest softest gown you can imagine, trimmed with silver fox—that's not really hot, you know—with a fluffy sort of bonnet to match. Oh, you can't think how well it suits Bertha's hair."

"I can quite believe it, dear," said Mrs. Weagles with earnest conviction. "She'll make a handsome bride, she will, and she has one great advantage, Julia, my dear—one very great advantage which she ought to be really thankful for—her nose never gets red. Ah well, my love, if I wasn't so much of an invalid, I'd be looking in and seeing all the pretty things. Never mind, I've a deal to amuse me, and this is a nice cheerful house to live in."

As she spoke, the old lady, drawing her shetland shawl about her shoulders, leaned forward and gazed again into the looking-glass.

"They're out of sight," she said a little regretfully; "I suppose they are gone for a walk, poor dears. Well, it's a nice day, though cold."

Like the Lady of Shalott, (though unlike that heroine of romance in many material points) Mrs. Weagles saw

> ". . . moving thro' a mirror clear
> That hangs before her all the year,
> Shadows of the world appear."

And even as for the Lady of Shalott, a crisis was impending for her. She clasped her hands eagerly as she exclaimed :

"My love, here's Dr. Jackson coming! I've not seen him for centuries!"

"Dr. Jackson!" exclaimed Aggie in surprise.

"Yes, he's positively flying along. Why, what can the dear man be after ? Just as if he were tramping through the city on business! Oh, it's perhaps your sister's house he's coming to! Well, no wonder, for it *is* a long, long time since he called. Has he an appointment, my love ?"

" No, that is, I—I think not," said Aggie.

"He ought to be ashamed of himself," continued Mrs. Weagles with rapidity. "Do you know I used at one time to think—well, never mind—why, he's passed your door— he'll be passing mine! Quick, quick, child ! Open the window, and call him in ; it's quite an easy catch—such a light pane, dear, pull it ! Quick, quick !"

Meanwhile, the object of Mrs. Weagles' interest was in truth speeding along, swinging his cane, his hat pulled down over his brows, and his eyes fixed on the pavement, looking neither to the right nor to the left. It seemed as though, necessity forcing him to pass a certain fateful house, he was deter-

mined to do so as quickly, as defiantly, and
with as little appearance of friendliness as
possible.   Aggie, struggling with the window
latch, which despite Mrs. Weagles' commen-
dation proved at first refractory, could get
no glimpse of Dr. Jackson's face, but came
to the conclusion that his figure was as
thick-set as ever, and his shoulders a little
more hunched up than usual.   Meanwhile,
the slight noise proceeding from the window
made the young man look up suddenly.
A thunderbolt would not have induced him
to raise his eyelids towards Bertha's abode,
but he had almost thought his danger over-
past.   As he glanced up quickly now, his
eyes met Aggie's in full.   There was but a
narrow space between Mrs. Weagles' bay-
window and the pavement — so narrow a
space that the child's bright head seemed
close indeed, with some locks of fair hair
blowing out towards him from the open pane,

and a flash of sky-blue—his favourite colour —about the neck and shoulders.

With a nod that was almost discourteous the young man was about to pass on, (nay, he had already passed in a shorter space of time than it has taken his chronicler to indite the fact,) when Aggie called to him to stop. She had been very unwilling to do so, but Mrs. Weagles, who foresaw the possibility of an interesting scrap of conversation, repeated energetically :

" Call him, my love, call him, call him ! "

The young man paused, irresolute. Then, somewhat to Aggie's surprise he retraced his steps. He even raised his hat with some politeness, as he came close under the window.

" Did you need anything, Miss Julia ? " he asked gravely.

" Mrs. Weagles wants you," replied Aggie ; " come in, please."

Her face was burning with blushes, and she was glad to draw in her head precipitately and retreat to the other end of the room, where her zeal with regard to Mrs. Weagles' knitting afforded her a comfortable shelter—physical and mental also.

Dr. Jackson stood yet doubtful, his hand on the open gate—then apparently making up his mind he ran quickly up the stone steps, and knocked at the door. Susan, who shared some of her mistress' proclivities, and was seldom out of the way of any gossip, opened the door immediately and ushered the visitor in.

"Dear! dear! Dr. Jackson!" exclaimed Mrs. Weagles. "Why, you *couldn't* have passed my door without coming in, surely! It's not a minute since I was telling my little friend Julia how much I wanted to see you, all along of a grandchild of a sister of mine—and Julia, here, she was looking out of the window as girls will, with nothing whatever to do, and so she said to me all of a sudden: 'Why, Mrs. Weagles, here's our dear Dr. Jackson coming down the road.'"

Aggie, who was well used to her old friend's exaggerations, and knew that, through haste of language and overflowing kindly curiosity, the dear old dame was scarcely cognizant that she sometimes wandered from the strict path of truth—Aggie did not even look up from her knitting. Dr. Jackson remained standing, hat in hand, poking at the floor with the end of his cane.

"Well, here I am, my dear madam," he said at last; "what do you want of me?"

"My dear doctor! What do I want! Why, ever so much!"

"I—I'm in a hurry to-day," said the young man, taking out his watch. "I have a most important engagement."

"Then tell me all about it!" cried Mrs. Weagles, clasping her hands comfortably. "Sit down. This is a most comfortable armchair. Now, Dr. Jackson, I call this *really* friendly of you—it is positively delightful. Have you something very, *very* dreadful? Oh, I do hope not," continued the interrogator with increased sympathy; "is it a serious case? Oh, if you look like that, I am sure it must be something awful!"

The young man, though he had mechanically taken the proffered seat, felt himself suddenly recalled to the absurdity of his position.

"My dear Mrs. Weagles," he said with a short laugh," I am sure you must know that I never talk about my patients—no medical man worth a brass farthing ever does."

"No, no, of course not, and medical gentlemen are worth a great many farthings sometimes, aren't they?" asked the old lady in a wheedling tone.

"Yes, I suppose so," replied the young man without the expected smile. His eyes strayed in the direction of Aggie, whose face was only partly turned away from him.

"How like Bertha she grows," he thought, viewing her all the more tenderly for the thought. And, despite a pang of bitter regret, he seemed mentally to slip into a sudden sense of ease and well-being—that sense which we experience when we meet something (long missed) that was a familiar happiness, and we walk again in old customary paths of pleasantness. If Aggie were not Bertha, she was certainly the very nearest thing to Bertha in the whole world:

"Si ce n'est pas la rose, elle a vécu près d'elle."

Edward Jackson became gradually conscious of the soothing influence stealing over him. Perhaps after all it was like that delightful absence from pain which follows pain, and is happiness in itself just because it is not pain.

He sat on, hearing the old lady's voice as we hear a running rivulet; consciously, yet without disconnecting any one note of sound from another. In plain English, he did not object to her talk, but he was not listening.

"Silver fox," Mrs. Weagles repeated. " Or was it grey fox ? No, I am sure, quite sure—Julia, my love, you did say silver fox, didn't you ? "

The young doctor roused and shook himself, and gave a short cynical laugh.

"Grey fox," he said meaningly. " Well, Mrs. Weagles, " I must wish you a very good morning."

"Oh, don't go!" pleaded the old lady entreatingly.

" But I must. If I had only time, you

may be quite sure I should want to hear
a great many more details about that lordly
grey fox."

The old lady looked up, slightly bewildered.

"*Silver* fox, indeed, doctor. Well, if you
must, you must. Good-bye. Julia, my dear,
will you shut the front door gently after Dr.
Jackson? I saw Susan cross the street a
moment ago."

Aggie rose reluctantly, and followed the
young man out of the room. As soon as the
two were alone in the passage, the expression
of his face suddenly changed. Aggie could
see that he was haggard and looked ill.
There were drawn lines of pain about his
eyes. Very gently he took both her hands:

"Tell me how she is?" he whispered
eagerly. "Is she happy?"

And Aggie heard herself saying, for her
own voice seemed changed:

"Yes, I think so."

" Tell her," began the young man, speaking very low, " tell her——"

But, quite suddenly, his eyes shone with a strange brightness—surely there were tears standing in them. He dropped the child's hands, and turned away. He quickly opened the door of the house to escape, but Aggie caught his arm :

" Tell her *what ?*" she asked in agitation ; "yes, you must say! Tell her——"

" Nothing," said the young man shortly.

" Oh yes, something," entreated the child.

She clung with all her might to his arm, and spoke with intense earnestness. Her fervour seemed to communicate itself to her listener.

"Well then, this ; tell her that I would do anything in the world for her."

The child's lips parted to speak, but he would not hear. He shook his head. She had already asked too much.

Hurriedly he drew his arm from her slackened grasp, and ran down the steps and walked quickly away, without looking round. Aggie, who was afraid of Mrs. Weagles' scrutinizing eyes, wandered bareheaded along the street in an opposite direction to that which he had taken. She was not sorry to meet Susan, and to help her to carry home a whole armful of seed-cake and crumpets for afternoon tea.

CHAPTER XII.

IT was the eve of the wedding-day, and Bertha and her sister were to spend it alone. Even Lord Delachaine had been forbidden the house after five o'clock. This had been Aggie's special fancy, her special prayer, the one thing which in all these latter days of renunciation she had clung to with a tenacity of purpose from which nothing could turn her. She and Bertha were to spend their last evening together. The earl and his sister had suggested a family dinner-party, a banquet at which all the members of the house of Delachaine were to meet. Aggie would of course be present, and any friends or relations of the Millings' would be duly

invited, including a distant cousin—so distant
that Bertha herself had never seen him but
twice in her life before, but who had under-
taken a long journey in order to give away
the bride.

But Aggie would have none of it. Bertha
had unreservedly promised her the gift of
this last evening, and assuredly a family
dinner-party in Belgrave Square—with the
joys of which she was already acquainted—
was by no means to Aggie's taste.

Lord Delachaine, slightly "huffy," had at
last proposed an evening at the play, but
no, this was not to be heard of. Even
Bertha herself had somewhat nervously hinted
that her little sister was bent upon what
might become almost a painful pleasure.
Bertha would have fain implied—yet scarcely
dared to do so—how that protracted leave-
takings are a kind of self-torture which we
should wisely omit in this world, where there

are already many more prickles than smooth places.

Jemima was perhaps the only person who thoroughly entered into Aggie's plan. In carrying it out the child had yielded to what was not a callous selfishness. During the last few weeks, her conduct had been persistently self-denying; for that very reason she was all the more overwhelmed by a desire to push away the inevitable for one brief moment, before it had become the irrevocable, and to forget likewise the immediate past, so as to live the lovely old life once again, if only for the space of that short evening.

It was a delusion, of course ; no one knew this better than Aggie herself, yet she wanted to 'make believe' as children do in lesser things. Despite the womanly side of her nature she was in many things very childish. Nor, for the matter of that, do some people

ever outgrow the infantine wish to make
believe.

Bertha's diamond and sapphire ring flashed
annoyingly into Aggie's eyes as she sat on
a low stool at her sister's feet, leaning her
head (as had been her wont of old) upon
Bertha's soft gown, and caressing with her
eager little hands Bertha's indolent white
fingers. There was no stain of paint nor perfume of turpentine upon these now. Bertha's
very self seemed changed to the child's
jealous eyes, and yet, to a casual observer,
Bertha would have appeared as much as
ever the mistress of the studio in which
she sat.

The carefully-dusted easels had been
pulled forward and laden with pictures so
as to furnish the centre of the room; the
afternoon sun, admitted by the garden door,
flickered instead of firelight on numerous
unfinished works and on the well-worn folds

of the ragged tapestry. A comfortable tea-
table was placed by the fireplace which, like
the table, was loaded with flowers so as to
present as festive an aspect as possible. Yet
everything was disappointing! Even the
sunshine and the flowers brought sadness
to Aggie's heavy heart. To her, the dingy
surroundings of former times, and the very
darkness of a winter's day, would have been
in truer harmony. Aggie would have liked
a brown fog, or at least pouring rain. And
yet perchance Bertha was happier now than
she had ever been. The room was strewn
with Lord Delachaine's gifts. (Aggie had
removed all other wedding-presents, but had
not dared to meddle with these.) And
the roses which the child had bought and
arranged, blooming around Bertha verily
suited that pretty person who, in her dainty
gown, with the pink hues of health and peace
upon her cheeks, was not unlike a rose

herself. She was about to be transplanted
to a more congenial soil, no doubt—she
seemed to take very kindly to her new
glories. An almost savage and very unusual
desire to inflict just an infinitesimal amount
of pain on her calm sister, to prick her out
of her contentment for a moment, rose up
violently in the very midst of Aggie's
despondency, But no, it must be all sunshine and roses now; there was not even
a thorn visible amongst the latter.

The wedding-day had been necessarily
postponed, owing to the death of old Lady
Delachaine's brother. He was the head of
his house, and therefore must be treated with
due respect, even after his demise. Consequently, the marriage was put off for awhile,
and as Bertha objected to the ill-luck of
being married in May, the ceremony could
not take place till June. Yes, this was June,
the month of roses, the month when the very

earth wears a perfumed garlanded robe, when daylight hours are long and sweet, and birds sing ceaselessly. . . .

"Do you remember," asked Aggie plaintively, "do you remember that afternoon when we sat like this, you and I? You had just finished your work—it was dark and chilly—we were toasting muffins—Lord Delachaine came—do you remember, Booffles? It seems so long ago."

"Yes," replied Bertha with a smile; "of course I remember, dear."

"I wonder if you ever knew—I smeared a wee atom of turpentine on his muffin," said Aggie laughing in spite of herself, "to see if he cared for you—he wouldn't have eaten it if he hadn't cared. How silly it was—how could I be such a goose!"

"How could you be such a goose?" repeated Bertha vaguely, stroking the fluffy hair that lay across her knee.

"It seems so long, so very long ago," repeated Aggie.

"Suppose we go into the kitchen and make some toast now?" said Bertha, jumping up.

That evening drew to a close, as all such evenings must, heavily and flatly. Both girls were glad when early bedtime drew near. Perchance, had Aggie been older and wiser she would not have risked the experiment of those last few hours, yet in days to come she often turned back to them in thought lingeringly and lovingly, for was not Bertha still all her own on that wedding eve?

It was summer twilight when the sisters went upstairs together at last, hand in hand, arm over arm. Everything had been discussed and re-discussed. It was settled that on the morrow Aggie was to take up her residence for a couple of weeks with old Mrs. Weagles, whilst Jemima took charge of

Bertha's house and Bertha's things. On that eventful morrow the bridal pair were to travel down to Delachaine Court, there to spend some days. This had been the earl's special wish, and Bertha had not contradicted it. He wished her to like the place from the very first, he had said, and Bertha had smiled, acquiescing graciously in this expectation of the future. Lord Delachaine had also expressed his desire to be as much as possible alone with his bride; he had not mentioned Aggie, but it was tacitly understood by every one that the child was not to reside with her sister for some time, nor to accompany her on the foreign trip which was agreeably to prolong the honeymoon. It was an equally tacit understanding that Aggie should, later on, take up her abode under Bertha's roof.

Meanwhile, it had been the child's own choice to go next door for the present. She

had received several other invitations. Even
the duchess had pleaded that Aggie might
come and stay with her during the first
separation from one who had been mother
as much as sister. Aggie, however, was
reprehensibly devoid of worldly considera-
tions, and preferred to avail herself of her
old neighbour's homely hospitality.

"You see, Booffles," the child had said in
explanation, " Mrs. Weagles wants me, and
I can do lots of things for her. I don't
know how it is, but I never feel half so
lonely when I am doing something for
people. I shall be able to put her quite
straight with her knitting, and clear up lots
of things about the neighbours, and make
much better tea than Susan can make, and
help to settle the bills, and see that Susan's
wages are paid up to the right date. There's
no end to all I can do!"

Aggie had said all this days ago. At the

time, when she had finished her speech, tears
had come into her eyes with a rush, and
a great lump had risen in her throat, so that
she had only had time to throw her arms
round Bertha's neck and give her a violent
hug, and dash hastily out of the room.

Now, as she went upstairs for the last
time to her sister's small simply-furnished
bedroom, Aggie was thinking of something
quite different. She was thinking of Dr.
Jackson's words. " Tell her," he had said,
" tell her, tell her——" What ? " Nothing."
Yes, something — and she had told that
something to the best of her ability to Bertha.
She had not told it at once ; she had felt it
would be so useless. The young lover's
words were like the jarring notes of some
half-forgotten melody. Of old the accompani-
ment had befitted those words, harmonized
with them and helped them by pleasant
chords and echoes of themselves ; to-day, it

was struck in a strange key, and the discord
was a harsh one.

Aggie had hesitated to apprize Bertha of
her interview with Dr. Jackson, and had put it
off from day to day, knowing that she must
tell. It was only this evening that she had
summoned up courage to confide in Bertha
sufficiently to give her a detailed narrative
of the short interview. She blamed herself
much, poor child, that she had not done so
sooner, but that was surely unnecessary.
When she had come to the difficult conclusion, Bertha had patted her hand, saying :

" Yes, darling; and he said that? It was
very kind of him, wasn't it ? "

" No, it was not kind," thought Aggie, but
she did not know how to express herself, so
she kept silence, but a moment later she
asked timidly, hiding her head as she did so
in the soft folds of her sister's gown :

" Would it have made any difference

to you, Booffles dear, if I had told you sooner?"

"No, dearie, assuredly not; how should it?" was Bertha's placid answer.

So Aggie's uneasy conscience had been comforted, yet Dr. Jackson's words remained in her memory, however anxiously she strove to be rid of them.

When she entered Bertha's room, a sudden shock awaited her, for on the bed lay stretched out the white satin wedding-gown, wreath and veil all complete.

"Oh, come into my room," said Aggie hurriedly.

The wedding-gown had no part in her programme for the evening. This was what she had planned, and what followed: that Bertha was to undress her and hear her prayers just as when she was a little child, and help her into her little white bed, and tuck her up, and put her arms round her with mother's and sister's love all in one, and then, whilst Aggie's golden head lay on the pillow and her two hands were clasped, that Bertha should repeat softly the old dearly-loved familiar lines :

> " Four corners to my bed,
>   Six angels round my head ;
>   Two to pray, two to wake,
>   Two to guard me till day-break.
>   Matthew, Mark, Luke, and John,
>   Bless the bed that I lie on."

After this repetition of an old custom was over on this memorable evening, there was a long silence. The lights were out, the fire was nearly out also. In the darkness each sister felt the loving tender presence of the other, could hear the soft breathing, and the beating of each other's hearts, and knew, without speaking, what each other's thoughts might be.

At last Aggie spoke :

" Booffles," she said, very softly, " you

know that if I could have prevented—I mean
if I could ever prevent anything bad from
happening to you, I would give my life very,
very willingly."

"I know," answered Bertha brokenly,
"and you know, Aggie, you know, my dear
little Agamemnon, that I would do anything——"

"Yes, I know," said Aggie sitting up in
bed and drawing her sister yet closer, "you
would come, you said—you said you would
come!"

"Of course I would come," replied Bertha,
trying to steady her voice; "don't let us
excite ourselves—indeed, darling, there is no
need. It is—it is——"

"Is it happiness?" asked Aggie, wonder-
ingly.

"It is——" began Bertha tremulously, but
she could not say the word. She broke
down into a perfect passion of tears. She

could not speak the word happiness. She was not like Aggie ; she dared not pause to think. She could not bear to be asked questions, nor to ask herself questions. All had seemed bright but a short time ago— this was darkness and nervousness—surely to-morrow would bring sunshine and security !

So the two girls wept for a while in each other's arms, and then they parted for the night, with many kisses, but no more speeches, no more protestations nor explanations.

As Bertha went down the chilly passage to her own room the clock struck twelve. It was midnight, then—nay, already the beginning of her wedding-day.

She shuddered as she went softly into her own bower. The moonlight was shining on the wedding-dress. She took it hastily from the bed and placed it on a chair beside. Then she lay down, thankful to seek oblivion in sleep.

CHAPTER XIII.

THE Duke of Baynham could make no
progress in his literary work. All the
morning he had struggled with unaccountable
difficulties. Meanwhile, as was his invariable
custom when in perplexity, he paced rest-
lessly up and down his study. Indeed, he
had long since actually worn a perceptible
path in the Turkey carpet, by dint of pacing
to and fro. Many a day was spent thus, his
hands in the pockets of an old shooting-coat,
his head thrown back, and his eyes staring
up at the ceiling.

The duchess, though she outwardly
lamented the maltreatment of the carpet,
inwardly rejoiced at her husband's propensity.

"It gives him so much exercise," she would often say; "poor dear Cas! Why, if he were always to sit doubled over Dante, he would grow hollow-chested, which would make me miserable; he might also get a dreadful liver complaint, which would make him miserable."

And so the duke, as blessedly ignorant of the wear and tear of the carpet as of his wife's comments thereon, pursued the even tenour of his way.

On this particular day, however, even peripatetic philosophy failed to benefit his authorship. He was tired, possibly; the wind was blowing from the east, and east winds, "good for neither man nor beast," were his particular aversion. He paused more than once on his monotonous march to push the logs of his summer wood-fire more closely together in the grate. In one of these pauses he noticed, with sudden dismay,

a tray which the butler had brought in an
hour previously and dexterously balanced
on two chairs. (The tray had been thus
judiciously supported because, although there
were several large tables in the room, there
was not one on which could be seen a square
foot of clear space, nor where any of the
heaped-up octavos and duodecimos might be
disturbed, without risk of drawing down on
the disturber sundry unexpected tomes, to
say nothing of their owner's suppressed but
none the less alarming vials of wrath.)   On
the tray were a couple of silver dishes.   In
the centre of one reposed two cutlets, once
hot, now cold and cheerless-looking, and
surrounded by a thin and fatty film that
should have been gravy.   Within the second
dish a few potatoes leaned forlornly against
each other.   The duke stared at this unin-
viting repast for a moment, then went on
his way unconcernedly.   Just then the door

opened softly, and a pretty brown head shoved itself deprecatingly through the aperture, accompanied by a soft rustling sound of satin and velvet.

"Are you disposed to interview your Beatrice?" asked a sweet mocking voice. "Here I am, Cas, home much earlier than you expected, aren't I ?"

"Come in!" replied the duke laconically. He did not smile, but the furrows passed away from his forehead as his wife entered. She was exceedingly smartly arrayed, from the tips of her dainty boots to the aigrette that swayed in her bubble of a bonnet.

"Dear, dear!" she exclaimed; "what a pity it is you have no looking-glass! I have heard so much about my dress this morning that I am positively pining to contemplate myself again. Cas dear, do you think I *could* manage, like Narcissus or whoever it was, to see myself in the shining back of one of your old books ?   No, I fear not ; there's too much dust everywhere, and of course nothing to wipe the dust off with in this wretched room."

The duke sighed abstractedly.   He was turning over the leaves of his manuscript.

" Are you busy, dear ? " asked the duchess gently.

" No; for once I am quite glad to be interrupted, Mary.   But if you call yourself Beatrice I must say I don't think Dante's lady-love wore such fine feathers as these."

" But would he not have liked her to, Cas ? That is the question.   Though :

> 'Think you, if Laura had been Petrarch's wife,
> He would have written sonnets all his life?'"

" No, indeed," replied the duke, smiling.

" Never mind ; only think how, if Laura *had* been Petrarch's 'haus-frau,' she could have helped the poor dear by sorting and arranging the sonnets he addressed to other people, imaginary people, I mean, tidying them, copying them out, etc., etc. That's where we come in so useful. But seriously, Cas, you are too ignorant. I mean to start a gazette of fashion all by myself for your sole benefit."

" The number of copies sold will scarcely repay the expense of publication," said the duke drily.

"Oh dear no," answered the duchess complacently. She was sitting, according to her wont, at the end of the sofa, rocking herself to and fro, and occasionally tapping the floor with her heels. Truly, this familiar attitude had been partly acquired through sheer necessity—the actual seat of the wide and comfortable sofa being as completely covered with books as were the tables in the room.

" I can assure you," continued the speaker, eyeing her lord and master with some dignity, " I can assure you that by next week there will be paragraphs in the *Court Circular*, the *Lady's Arcadia*, and a few other well-known papers, very much to this effect :

" ' At the wedding of the young and lovely Countess of Delachaine, we noticed with interest that one of the most beautiful and striking costumes was worn by the charming Duchess of Baynham.' Now, Cas, why don't *you* pay me a compliment ? "

The duke who, with an air of fatigue, was leaning against an unbook-cased place in the wall, now roused himself and smiled affably in answer. He clasped his hands behind his head, and stood watching his wife in thoughtful silence.

" You are lamentably uninterested. Can you say nothing ? " she asked with just severity. " Before I move from here, I mean to make you tell me how I look."

" You look exceedingly tidy."

" Is that all ? "

"That is all."

But though his words were scant, it is to be presumed that the duchess read between the narrow lines. She jumped down from her perch, and, running to her husband, knelt hastily beside him. Thereupon, possessing herself of one of his hands, she rubbed her own soft cheek against it, murmuring in a low tone which contained but little disapproval :

"You dear old thing! You very dear old thing! Now I will tell you all about the wedding."

"Oh, to be sure!" remarked the duke suddenly awakened; "it is poor Delachaine's wedding-day, so it is! And how did he get through it, eh? Was he turned off all right?"

"My dear Cas! Why, you forget! You were ill—it was quite impossible for you to go—and I made your excuses to the whole family. Don't you remember what you told me this morning ? "

" Of course, of course ! I had a terrible threatening of influenza this morning."

" No, it was not influenza," quoth the duchess with decision. " It was a violent headache; a very severe and sudden head-ache. I hope you will stick to that, Cas, if you see Aunt Mary or Dosia or any of them. Because," she added aggrievedly, " you really did say you had a headache, and I really did believe you."

" Yes," answered the duke in a contrite tone, " I remember now. Besides, I have a headache at the present moment—I have. I assure you. Well, was the bride lovely ? "

" She looked very pretty, and self-possessed. Oh so self-possessed, you can't think ! With hectic spots on her cheeks like the people in books, and a train five yards long. But, Cas, it was little Julia—that dear little Julia

—who took my thoughts away. I felt I must jump up and kiss her all the time the Bishop was telling us how to behave to our husbands."

" You looked upon her as a sort of proxy, I hope."

" Not at all ; it was entirely for her own dear sweet delightful little self. Of course you know she was Bertha's only bridesmaid, and she was dressed in a soft limp white muslin Sir-Joshua-kind of frock with a broad pale blue sash and a mob cap, and her hair— you remember her hair, Cas ?—floating out in all manner of directions."

" You're an admirable hand at description, Mary !"

" Well, I'm your only chance of gaining information, so you'd better be kind to me. I must tell you that little Julia wore the row of pearls John sent her—you know he gave her the prettiest tiny row of pearls in the

world, and a big posy of white flowers—
simple sort of things."

" Poor old John! And how did he bear
himself ? "

"Well," replied the duchess with a spice
of malice, "all the ladies said he looked
very stately. That is the only remark I
heard. But he really was most kind and
obliging and took care of lots of people ; in
fact but for him I should have got squeezed
to death in the crush. You know there
was a sort of cold collation in the studio, not
a stand up nor a sitting down breakfast."

" What, not a sitting down *nor* a stand
up ? " repeated the duke, bewildered.

" How silly you are, Cas! I mean everything on trays and in odd corners, don't you
know ? With bits of curtains and pots, and
nice polite maids in caps."

"Ah, I see! And how did Dosia look ? "

" As cross as ten toads."

"Are toads cross? That is a curious statement relative to natural history. And how about the jewel in their heads?"

"Aunt Mary cried, of course, nearly all the time, and dropped her handkerchief and mopped her eyes with her gloves. I suppose she felt it was quite good-bye to John."

"And to Belgrave Square."

"There were some nice girls who had been fellow-students with Bertha at the Slade School, and a good many of her friends came one way or another. The President was there in full force, and some very picturesque people. The Delachaine family naturally mustered strong—there were the Boltons, and the Winchcotes and the Asbreys——"

"And the Piccaninnies and the Joblillies, I suppose, all complete."

"Do you think, Cas, that John himself might be called the 'great Panjandrum'?

He did not look unlike it to-day, I assure
you.   It was quite the first time in my life I
have ever seen him in such new clothes."

" Did he cry ? "

" Only his mother wept, as I told you.
No one else shed a tear.   As for that dear
darling little Julia, when Lord and Lady D.
had driven away, she stood watching the
carriage, looking like a figure of stone; really,
Cas, I do assure you, my heart bled for
her ! "

" I can easily believe it, my dear !   Your
heart—— "

" Nonsense, nonsense, I am not such a
fool as you think !   Now I must leave you
and undress."

" What, take off all those fine feathers ? "

" Yes.   I have to attend a committee."

" Oh—a committee ! "

" Certainly, a committee.   It is the working committee for friendless orphans."

The duke, who had by this time mentally travelled back to his Dante, and had consequently again commenced to pace up and down the room, smiled at these words.

" My dear Mary, did you ever hear of the man who murdered both his parents, and, at his trial, pleaded that he was an orphan ? "

" *Really*, Cas ! "

This indignant remark bore no relation to the duke's time-honoured anecdote, however. The duchess, with a look of horror, was pointing to the luncheon tray and the two chilly cutlets :

" Is that—*that* your lunch ? " she asked, authoritatively.

" My dear," faltered the duke, suddenly grown timid and abashed, " it was—that is to say I—I really—— "

" I shall order you some hot grilled chicken at once," said his wife, stalking with dignity to the door.

" Pray don't; my dear girl—the servants —they will all be so put out ! "

" But *I* am put out," cried the duchess flying from him, and shutting his own door in his face.

She had a short but pithy interview with the butler, after which her quick feet carried her upstairs to her bedroom, where she exchanged her robes of magnificence for a plain stuff gown, with a jacket to match and a tight little black straw bonnet and veil.

She was bent upon attending a charitable committee of which she was one of the most zealous members, and for the meeting of which she was already belated. Yet, during the whole time that she was dressing, she was haunted by Aggie's set white face. The kindly duchess was conscious of an ardent impulse which filled her mind, and intensified every moment—an impulse to seek out the child on this day of desolation, when for the first time in Aggie's young life the poor little thing had sustained a definite parting from her beloved sister.

As the duchess terminated the task of buttoning her gloves (and she was very particular anent those buttons) she reflected that occasions might arise in life when it would be a truer mercy to visit and cheer one solitary orphan than to sit at a green baize table with other ladies to discourse on the food and clothing of some fifty orphans, poorer perhaps than Aggie, yet surely not more sorrowful.

The duchess was delighted when she arrived at this sensible solution of her perplexities. Seldom are duty and inclination permitted to go hand in hand; whenever they do so our satisfaction overflows to such a degree that we are firmly convinced we have never followed the path of duty thus truly before. It was with a genuine throb of

joy that the duchess pattered quickly downstairs, and out into the street, where she
hailed a hansom, and bade the driver hasten
on the way.

CHAPTER XIV.

Mrs. Weagles' maid Susan was standing
at the open front-door telling the fish-
monger's boy a great many details concerning the wedding. Susan, unlike the duchess,
had not thought fit to doff her wedding
garments, and, as she had been one of the
neat handmaidens in caps flippantly alluded
to by a certain narrator, she presented
a holiday appearance which was further
enhanced by the elegant knot of white satin
and orange flower, with silver leaves, which
she wore just below her collar. Susan was
fatigued and flustered by the events of the
morning, though also proud of being a
participator in what was certainly the great

event of the neighbourhood.   There was
a sort of reflected glory from the wedding
cast on Mrs. Weagles' house and Mrs.
Weagles' servant beyond what could fall on
any other house or servant in that street.
Moreover, was it not almost a badge of
honour that the sweet young lady, Miss Julia
Millings, sister of the bride—that bride who
was now the Right Honourable the Countess
of Delachaine, and who had gone off quite
high and grand-like in a beautiful carriage of
her own with two splendid big bay horses
and a coachman and powdered footman (not
to forget the bridegroom, who went off also)
—was at this very moment a guest residing
under the narrow but distinguished roof of
the said Mrs. Weagles ?

Susan did not recognize in the quietly-
dressed lady, who leaped lightly from the
hansom and ran up the steps of the house,
the duchess whose sumptuous clothing and

high position she had not yet grown weary of eulogizing, but it was with a gratified toss of her head that she flung open the parlour door and announced the distinguished visitor.

Mrs. Weagles was somewhat startled. Tired by the sight of the gay folks whom she had seen pass to and fro in her looking-glass, and furthermore exhausted by several lengthy descriptions of the festivities to which she had attentively listened, she was now dozing and gently nodding in her arm-chair, with a large piece of wedding-cake and other dainties placed in a dish close beside her. The old lady awoke with alacrity, however, and, like most somnolent people, asserted that she had not been asleep at all, but was only resting.

She found herself immediately placed at ease by the gracious simplicity of the daughter of the St. Phippens. It was really quite an after-thought in the good lady's mind that this delightful visit was a root, so to speak, from which might spring countless and most gratifying hours of gossip to cheer many dull future days.

" Julia is up-stairs," said Mrs. Weagles after the few first words of polite greeting; " shall I send for her ? "

" Oh no; please let me run up to her," said the visitor. " I see your maid in the passage ; may I ask her the way ? "

And off ran the duchess to inform herself as to Aggie's whereabouts; then, going upstairs alone and very softly, she knocked gently at the door of the child's bedroom.

" Come in," said Aggie.

She had heard a hansom draw up to the door, and was aware of the sound of voices downstairs, for the house was by no means a large one. But, unlike Mrs. Weagles, being singularly deficient in curiosity, Aggie had not stirred to make any enquiry.

Moreover, she was fairly overcome with the grief of losing her sister. She could not cry. She had not shed a tear during the whole day, but her head and heart and limbs ached heavily and painfully, and the chill desolation that had taken possession of her seemed to creep closer and closer, surrounding and enveloping her so that there seemed to be no escape from it. Now that Bertha was gone, there could no longer be any necessity for keeping up. The poor child still clung to her original idea that she might greatly benefit old Mrs. Weagles by her society, but that must be some other day, and the benevolent idea itself was not sufficient to chase away the utter dreariness which had fallen upon poor Aggie.

When the door opened, the child looked round without any apparent interest, but at sight of her visitor she jumped up with an exclamation of joy.

"Why, what *are* you about, here all by yourself?" asked the duchess, with as much playfulness as she could muster.

She advanced towards the table at which Aggie had been sitting. It was covered with fanciful paper and writing materials of all sorts. Aggie was not a brilliant scribe and it is well known that the least expert workmen require the best and greatest number of tools. Bertha had lavished these tools on her little sister. The ink was not yet dry at the bottom of a long scrawled page—a big page of highly ornamented paper.

"I am writing to Bertha," said the little girl simply.

"To Bertha? My dear child!"

There was a slight tinge of reproach in the tone of these words which Aggie was quick to perceive.

"I am not going to send the letter to-day," she said quietly. "I know it might vex

Bertha if she fancied I fretted too much. I only thought I would begin. I am going to write one sheet every day. It will be like a diary, and then, at the end of a few days, I shall have a really fat letter to send."

"You poor little thing!" exclaimed the duchess.

Aggie made a step forward, and laid her pale little face against the kindly shoulder that seemed pleasantly near, both literally and metaphorically ; then she slid one small cold hand into her friend's warm palm.

The latter had no children of her own, and it is generally supposed that the women who are mothers are those most surely drawn towards other people's children. But this is not always the case. Indeed, mothers are sometimes too apt to view their neighbours' offspring only in comparison or in opposition to their own, and, by very reason of an increasing home circle, to restrict an

interest which might otherwise have amiably
widened and strengthened. The childless
duchess, when confronted with a baby, could
neither hush nor dandle it. She was apt
merely to stroke its blossom-like cheek gently
with the tip of her little finger. But for all
sorrows, great or small, of this pulsating,
suffering world, for the sorrows of the young
especially perhaps, she had an intuitive and
generous sympathy. After all, it is tenderness, not maternity, which is the crowning
grace of womanhood.

As she looked into Aggie's face the duchess
grew very tender-hearted. She read an
almost cynical expression there which evoked
in her a desire to take the child to the nearest
church in order that her young sore spirit
might be soothed and elevated even whilst
it should be quieted. But she reflected that
Aggie had seen enough of church already
to-day. The garish ceremony of this very

morning must naturally prevent any such influence as she desired. For the moment— a mere moment, it was to be hoped—the sacred building might suggest only thoughts of unrest—smart gowns, excitement, an atmosphere not of peace, but of painful ceremonial.

Then an idea struck her.

" The next best thing to going to church," said the duchess to herself, "is assuredly to spend an hour in the National Gallery. Aggie," she continued aloud, " I want you to put on your hat and come out with me at once ; let us go and see some pictures."

" Pictures !" exclaimed Aggie with a little shudder.

She hardly liked to acknowledge to herself that her friend was not quite so considerate as usual. Pictures ! What, when Ruth and Boaz, and the Infant Samuel, and a score or two more such works were filling up Bertha's deserted bedroom and her own, (because the studio had to be cleared for the wedding feast,) their reproachful faces turned to the wall, or stacked one against the other!

The duchess blushed slightly as she guessed the poor child's train of thought.

" There are such different kinds of pictures," she stammered. " Have you ever been to the National Gallery ? "

" Never."

It was true that Aggie had spent all her short life in the centre of art, that is to say modern art. Nevertheless, poor Bertha was not a first-rate artist, nor had she perhaps ever violently struggled to become one. The end and object of her painting was to sell ; she had studied seriously but a few years, and she was more of a picture manufacturer (so said her critics) than a great artist in the truest sense of the word. Of old masters both here and abroad she knew comparatively little, scarce more indeed than the uncultivated Aggie. The walks of high art were fenced off from her mental view, and she never tried to stand on tiptoe. A pretty face, a bright piece of drapery, with just as much of back-ground as was absolutely necessary—these were to Bertha the chief requirements of a picture. Even Eldon was to her an enigma; much as she liked and respected him, there was something in his work as in his talk that was often utterly incomprehensible to her. So was it also with regard to the creations of several other eminent painters. Bertha knew that they were great men; she even claimed friendship with a few of them, but she was comfortably satisfied herself to seek a lower level than theirs. She shewed therein at least the wisdom which we do not all of us possess (a melancholy wisdom per-chance) of gauging the height and breadth of our own talent, or what we christen such.

Aware as she was that she could neither reach the sky nor encompass the sea, she never attempted impossible results, nor did she wear out her pretty eyes in crying for the moon.

"Well then, you must come, you certainly must come!" the duchess repeated, taking Aggie's hands in hers.

Mrs. Weagles' consent was not difficult to obtain, and, before many moments had passed, Aggie and her friend were seated in the hansom on their way to Trafalgar Square. Arrived at their destination, they went up the broad steps of the National Gallery hand in hand. To Aggie's sensitive mind, the hush and calm apparent immediately on entering the edifice were inexpressibly attractive. The very pictures themselves were different from those to which she was accustomed, and the glow of colour upon the walls, set in the mellow gilding of some fine old frames, pleased her fancy greatly.

The duchess cast a few anxious glances at her young charge, but her quick eyes soon discerned that all was well, and that she had not been mistaken in her prescription. For, although some folks require years of training and careful consideration, together with the earnest perusal of many stiff and learned books, before they can admire and enjoy the old masters, (especially what are denominated the early masters,) to others such appreciation comes spontaneously and is perhaps therefore all the more genuine and strong. To Aggie, whose nature, as the reader will already have perceived, was very different from that of her sister, the pictures now around her were a real and intense delight. Soon she grew positively excited, flitting about, and asking more technical questions than her companion's limited knowledge of painting could easily answer.

The duchess, on her part, was equally

delighted. Nay, she felt so kindly disposed to all the world because of the success of her small scheme that presently she began to take interest in a perfect stranger, a poor artisan evidently, who stood gazing at one of her favourite pictures with an unusually reverent expression on his aged face, and an eager light in his sad and sunken eyes.

"I really must go and speak to him!" exclaimed the duchess at last.

"Oh! Must you?" asked Aggie, slightly taken aback; then she added, somewhat nervously:

"May I sit here and wait?"

"Yes, dear, certainly," answered her friend smiling, and tripped off on her new mission.

The little duchess approached the working-man with this same confident smile. She felt that here was one of the interesting moments of her life: an experience which it was her distinct duty to go through; this untaught but appreciative son of the soil must assuredly be encouraged. Else, why did the radical writers write? Why had the judicious levelling of classes and masses been preached throughout the land? An artisan such as this, with a serious mind athirst for improvement and culture, was indeed a treasure not often trove.

In the warmth of her heart—and it was a very warm heart—all men and women were certainly equal before the presence of these great works teeming with subtle beauty and humanising art. Yet the little duchess was conscious of a slight tremor of nervousness which made speech more difficult than usual to her.

In truth, it is as difficult, when we feel things strongly, to urge our fellow-creatures along the path of culture as it is to pull them on in science, or shove them gently forward in religion. Our own enthusiasm and

honesty are not always sufficient to tell upon
others—not even though brought into play
for the noblest causes.

When the lady approached, the man
turned, glancing quickly at her for an instant,
then as quickly resuming his inspection of
the picture. He seemed to be studying it
deeply, yet with an obstinate independence
all his own. The duchess drew a step
nearer, so near indeed that, had she chosen,
she could have put her tiny gloved hand on
the rough frayed sleeve in front of her.
Then the man turned to her once more, and
very quietly he asked, moving aside as he
spoke :

"Did you want to see the picture, marm?"

"Thank you, thank you, I know it," said
the duchess nodding and smiling brightly ;
' I know it very well."

He looked at her, his grave face wearing
an expression of some surprise, and a hot

blush rose to hers, flooding it with crimson. She began to wish that she had not obeyed the philanthropic impulse which was already making her so exceedingly uncomfortable.

" It is a beautiful picture," she stammered.

" Beautiful," answered the stranger calmly, without moving or bowing, or giving expression to any of those practical and East-end observations she had somehow expected from him. Whereupon, with a feebleness of spirit which astonished herself afterwards, she murmured "good morning," and fled back to Aggie.

The duchess was very crestfallen after this failure, for so she viewed it. But Aggie was engrossed by the contemplation of the new world she had accidentally entered. The two friends passed from room to room, and lingered on. It was an effort to go forth again into the everyday world.

As they walked slowly and meditatively

down Pall Mall, they both kept silence.
Aggie was always wellnigh speechless when
she felt most deeply, and now her nature
was newly and strangely stirred. Pictures,
pictures, what were they? Something, perchance, of which she had never dreamed.
Surely they were books, written in a language
which each beholder must interpret for himself or herself. Or were they kind wise
counsellors who, knowing the sore place in
every one's heart, could touch it with gentle
healing, giving meanwhile, from the stores
of ancient learning, some message of perfect
truth ?

During this time, the duchess revolved in
her mind many theories and counter-theories.
All the power and practice of which, in her
secret heart, she had been very proud—the
power of influencing her fellow-creatures—
had failed her to-day, she scarce knew why.
Was it because, at that one moment, she had

acted rather upon book theory than by womanly feeling? Yet, as a rule, she blamed herself for acting too little according to judiciously-planned theories! Were all the pamphlets and dissertations of wise folks not so useful after all as they appeared, and was it possible that she had been carried away by a pragmatic desire to dissect a human being, instead of proceeding with the tactful intuition which was natural to her, and which had so seldom played her false?

She was very miserable about this little episode. She longed to run back and say to the working man:

" Sir, sir, I only wanted to help you. You see we both like the same Titian, the same Bellini!"

At last Aggie broke silence.

" Tell me," she asked very softly, " I want you to explain—there is something I don't understand, and you are sure to know."

"No, no," pleaded the duchess.

Aggie only shook her head. Some facts need little discussing.

"Tell me just one thing," she continued fervently; "why do all the faces that have the greatest pain in them seem the most beautiful? It is a beautiful pain which they seem to hold."

A curious sensation suddenly rose and tightened the throat of the duchess. Herein, then, this child understood her, felt with her, and went along with her. Yet, after her defeat, she felt oddly humbled, and unable to answer as she might otherwise have done.

"I—I am not sure that I can quite tell you, Aggie," she answered, even more softly than the child herself had spoken. They were walking very closely side by side, amongst the jostling pedestrians. "Some things are always mysteries—we understand them so little—and yet these very things are the truest foundations of our being. Like waves of sound, the vibrations of our deepest thoughts spread further than we think."

Aggie's face, in its unspoken sympathy, seemed to answer.

" I understand," she murmured.

The duchess flushed and went on almost feverishly :

"You ought to ask some one who knows better than I do—I am very sadly ignorant. Perhaps, perhaps the gospel of love is also that of pain ; perhaps, dear, the beauty you mean is something divine which we approach only occasionally—not often : the beauty of renunciation. Perhaps it is just because it is divine and rare that it means so much to us ; I do not know."

" There are so many perhapses in life," put in Aggie, with sad parenthesis.

" Cas might know," said the duchess.

CHAPTER XV.

The Earl of Delachaine was enjoying a short constitutional on the Riva dei Schiavoni. He had spent but a couple of hours at Venice, yet already the place seemed to him singularly wanting in those opportunities for exercise which he, as an Englishman, dearly appreciated. Whither, he wondered, should he presently go to stretch his legs?

Bertha was somewhat tired after a long journey, and was resting in her room, whilst her lord walked like a caged lion to and fro in the vicinity of the hotel, not wishing to investigate any of the historic buildings too closely without his wife's companionship. Up as far as the Piazzetta he wandered, back again past the hotel, and a few yards beyond, making his way with leisurely dignity in the midst of the noisy Venetian crowd, who, in truth, were not nearly so much surprised at the arrival of one tall dull-looking English-man the more as he was to find himself amongst such motley folk, watching their movements and gestures, and listening with-out comprehension to their quick and utterly bewildering jargon.

In his youth, the earl had acquired a few sentences of choice Italian. An admirable instructor—a trusty friend of his father's family, who came armed with a grammar, a dictionary, and a book of childish and point-less stories—had dinned into his unwilling ears some polite Tuscan phrases, whilst the recipient's thoughts were wandering lovingly in the direction of cricket or football. Need-less to say that such slight and long-vanished knowledge was but little use to the earl now in Italy, all the less at Venice. The only words he understood were the cries of ' acqua ' on the part of the brawny water-seller who elbowed past him, carrying heavy jars of drinking water for the benefit of fellow townsmen, and the insinuating offers of " gondola, gondola," from many gondoliers who were seemingly idling about, leaning over the parapet, or slumbering in shady corners, but who were none the less wide awake to their own interests, and seized, spider-like, the first opportunity of endeavouring to entrap so fine a new-comer into their floating parlours.

The earl stalked on, puffing slowly at his cigar, which the little Venetian arabs viewed with as much wonder as envy, for Italian cigars, though exceedingly lengthy, have not the breadth and general well-to-do appearance of those weeds habitually smoked by Lord Delachaine. The Doge's Palace, with its open archways revealing glimpses of the Giant's Stair, St. Mark's with its green bronze horses, the mighty Campanile, and the entrance to the Piazza, all looked alluring enough, but the earl turned his back resolutely on such glories, until he could enjoy them with Bertha.

As he retraced his steps again he came in view of the Bridge of Sighs. He could not fail to know that it was the Bridge of Sighs, for every one, from his landlord down to a ragged little boy—who could stand upon his head for a longer space of time than any other little ragged boy—had informed the earl that this was indeed the Bridge of Sighs ; even his own courier half an hour previously had chosen to emphasize the same statement.

Lord Delachaine searched in the recesses of his mind for some quotation from Byron or Rogers (he was not well up in more modern poets) concerning Venice and her interesting sights, but he sighed a little as he recognized how terribly short a portion of his life had been spent in the study of either poetry or art. Yet he was truly desirous of pleasing Bertha—Bertha was his, now, utterly and entirely his ; she had sacrificed much for him, her career, ay, and many friends who were doubtless more congenial to her refined and elevated spirit than he could ever hope to be.

Thus pondered the earl as he passed to and fro amongst the Venetian crowd. There was a perfect Babel of clamour and movement; laughter, music, argumentative angry voices, sounds of fun and ribaldry, the cackle of some old women, the street cries of the vendors of many wares, the chink of glasses from lemonade booths—above all the shrill whistle of the little Lido steamer. And beyond the gaily-dressed groups of girls, beyond the white paving-stones, and out towards lovely yellow San Giorgio opposite, glittered the rainbow-coloured dancing water, across which a few black gondolas were darting like swallows. It was a sight to make an artist paint, to bid a poet dream. To Lord Delachaine just then the beauty of the whole universe was summed up in one word—Bertha. He, the elderly man, seemed grave and uninteresting enough to the crowd about him ; people who are leading inner lives are seldom interesting to others. Yet this man was not dwelling in a fool's paradise. The lengthy honeymoon which he had himself urged had not yet wholly gone by ; and, whilst he was conscious that the love he bore his wife—a love of which he was almost ashamed as he considered his years—had strengthened and deepened every day, and was very strong within him, he was nowadays strangely diffident of his own worth and capability to please.

" She is so young," repeated Lord Delachaine to himself—" so fair—so young."

He said nothing more, even to himself ; it
was not his way to analyze things much.
Moreover, can one analyze happiness ?   Lord
Delachaine was well aware that he was very
happy.

He turned his steps towards the hotel.

The loungers, congregated about the
doorway, made room for the English earl.
Already his name and position were well
known, not only to the master of the hotel,
but to the humblest satellite thereof.   They
all hoped that his visit might not prove
a pecuniary disappointment to them.   They
greeted his approaching figure with affectionate eyes.   Meanwhile, " unconscious of
his fate," Lord Delachaine nodded with
suitable affability, threw away the end of his
cigar, and hurried in quickly and gaily,
mounting the stair rapidly and pushing

open the door of the large first-floor sitting-room.

As he entered in this haste, a pretty picture met his gaze. Bertha was sitting near the open window, through which poured a flood of southern sunshine. She was sitting with her back to the light, and the sunbeams glinted upon her hair, turning it into a golden nimbus, whilst the folds of her soft brown dress shone like molten gold. She was scattering breadcrumbs to a small company of pigeons who boldly surrounded her, three or four having entered the room, whilst others were still hesitatingly perched on the lovely white balcony between the arches of which shone glimpses of blue lagoon flecked with light, whilst overhead the sky glittered like a sapphire.

" Oh, isn't it delightful ! " she exclaimed, as Lord Delachaine entered. " These dear tame birds ! I had always heard of the pigeons of St. Mark—they are sacred, you know. Isn't it nice, John?"

"Yes, very," replied the earl meditatively; "but are you quite sure you won't catch cold, my love?"

"Oh no, how could I? Why, it is exceedingly hot."

"Treacherous, perhaps," said the earl, shaking his head.

"Where have you been, John? What did you see out?"

"Not much; only what you see from this window, and a good many dirty little boys besides. And it doesn't smell very fresh. But it will be pleasant to go with you by-and-bye, Bertha. Do you think you will like this place?"

"Oh yes!" answered Bertha quickly, to whom the idea of calling the Queen of the seas 'this place' seemed almost sacrilege. "It has always been my dream to come to Venice."

"Oh, that's all right then," answered the earl contentedly. He turned towards a table, whereon stood his crocodile-skin bag, a large despatch box, and a couple of ancient Galignanis. He took up one of the latter in some discontent.

"Giusti will be here directly with the letters," said Bertha, throwing a piece of bread in the direction of an enterprising pigeon who was artlessly roaming round one of his lordship's feet. "I am longing for the post. Surely it must be in by this time, John."

"I have ascertained that it arrives almost immediately, if it has not already come," said Lord Delachaine. "Giusti will bring us a good supply of newspapers at any rate, for I gave the address of the Poste Restante here for some days past."

"And I have not heard from Aggie for ever so long," said Bertha with a sigh.

"That is the worst of travelling—poor little Aggie!"

"I am not sure that she does not grudge you to me," said the earl slowly, as he threw away his paper and wandered to another window.

"Oh no, it is not grudging!" cried Bertha quickly. "My poor little Aggie!"

Even as she spoke, with an ominous tremor in her voice, the door opened and Giusti, the courier, entered the room, bearing a huge packet of letters and newspapers.

Giusti was a large swarthy man who spoke every language in a way—his way—but none with correctness or according to the traditions of orthodox grammarians. He wore rings, seals, and jewelled pins in profusion, and used pomatum and strong perfumes. His master was truly afraid of him, but nevertheless often tried to stem this son of Piedmont's flow of sentences by retreating within the shelter of austere and dignified brevity.

" Die post," said Giusti with unnecessary explanation ; then he proceeded to deal out the newspapers like playing cards :

"Vone, deux, trois, fors, cinque, sei, sette ; papairs, ecco ! Vone lettair for Miladi—voilà tout. Per Milor molto."

" Thank you, Giusti," said Lord Delachaine curtly.

" It is a most beautiful vedder. I have engage for Milor and Miladi a first-class gondola mit two gondolier. Vot time Miladi vish for dem ? "

" What time ? " asked Bertha vaguely, scarce understanding, and looking up from the solitary letter she had received, and which was to her as good as ten, being a voluminous packet of many sheets from Aggie.

" That will do, thank you, Giusti," said

Lord Delachaine majestically; "we will order the gondola presently."

"Ah! Bene, bene, parfaitement—as Milor voudra," quoth the retreating Giusti, and the earl, seating himself in what was the nearest approach to an easy-chair in the furniture of the room—though it was a seat that was excessively hard, with a straight back and a square shape, and no arms at all—proceeded to peruse his correspondence.

Occasionally, he cast a rapid glance in the direction of his wife, who had tucked herself up cosily near the window, which she had closed after chasing the pigeons away, and where she sat earnestly reading, her lap covered with thin blue sheets of letter-paper, scrawled and blurred over, whilst she smiled every now and then to herself with the happy colour rising to her cheeks, and her eyes seemingly brighter and her hair more feather-light and sunshiny than ever.

The earl's correspondence was of the most ordinary type. It was decidedly not amusing. The usual appeals from professional beggars were not wanting, nor yet circulars from hospitals and benevolent societies. Here was the customary annoying statement from the land agent regarding rents, repairs of farm buildings, etc. Next came a couple of bills, which Lord Delachaine viewed leniently enough, as they were "accounts delivered" of things supplied for his wedding-day, and these were supplemented by a letter from the son of his country curate wanting to know if his lordship would purchase a very fine St. Bernard puppy. The earl viewed his packet of correspondence with but slender gratitude. Finally, he took up with much unconcern a light and narrow letter which had been, like the rest, forwarded to Italy from Belgrave Square. He opened it carelessly, and nearly read the two short lines

through before he realized that he had read
them. For, indeed, his thoughts, vague as
they might be, were not unpleasant ones.
They stood between him and what had
hitherto been his dull home life, just as
Bertha's pretty golden figure shut out a
great part of the monotonous blue sea and
sky.

Suddenly—very suddenly—he was conscious of an acute pain that, strange to say,
was even more physical than mental. The
room seemed to reel around him, the sunshine to turn to gloom. The stone tracery of
the white balcony behind which he sat, the
mellow distance, the very air of the perfumed
south, nay more, even Bertha's radiant
presence—all seemed fast fading away. He
clutched at his chair, but almost instantly
recovered his outward composure, and clasped
his hands quietly, impressed curiously with
the idea that he must be strong and silent.

Yes, that was the one necessity : to be silent above all things, and next, not to mind over much.

This revolution of thought lasted but the space of a moment ; yet, during that short moment, the whole world changed for Lord Delachaine. He lived, it is true, and breathed, but it was in the dark, and through a mist of pain. The next moment, however, he shook himself together and smiled. A mental shock is often like a sudden eclipse. The absence of light is only for a short while. Of course this was just one of the things that happen every day, one of those things which—because they cannot be credited and have neither sense nor founda-tion—pass, and must needs be forgotten. So said Lord Delachaine to himself, and he repeated internally : Surely they leave no trace nor remembrance behind.

With clearness of vision and calmness of

heart, therefore, he proceeded to read the letter once more. It was short; its brevity perhaps too studied.

"Beware of Dr. Jackson," thus ran the words, "and believe

　　　　　　　"A WELL-WISHER."

Dr. Jackson! Who on earth was Dr. Jackson? And what on earth had Dr. Jackson to do with him, or—ay, there lay the sting—with Bertha? For the third time he conned those hateful words.

The earl sat on in silence during some minutes. He had folded the letter and placed it in the breast-pocket of his coat. He reasoned with himself as he did so. It was certainly not the first time in his life that he had received an anonymous letter, though fortune had happily been sparing to him in such gifts, and he had always put but slight value upon them. He argued now that the

. well-wisher was probably his greatest enemy, or Bertha's ; some one, perhaps, whom she had refused for his sake—and this was a very sweet thought to him.   Yet it was strangely bitter-sweet.   Of course he was not a young man any longer—he knew that well enough. And he was rich.   This large palatial room was cold, surely, extremely cold.   There is nothing like Italy for sudden changes of temperature, thought the earl—fever, ague, etc., are daily dangerous.   Possibly, he had caught a chill on the journey.

At that moment, along the corridor, came the hurrying steps and the loud voice of a German waiter.

" Piftek aux bommes pour teux—barfaite-ment—dout de suite."

Association of ideas is a curious thing.   In after years Lord Delachaine could never endure to hear a German waiter speak French.   On such foolish common trifles is the structure of our life's happiness built, for memory goes far to help to raise the building. Lord Delachaine never liked Venice. The climate, he said, was variable and deceptive; the hotels noisy—people always eating and drinking. How seldom do other folks know why we like or dislike a thing! How well for us is it that they cannot unravel the clue to our innermost feelings!

CHAPTER XVI.

AT last Bertha looked up—she had been studying her letter for a long time. Now she was laughing softly.

"I do think," she began, "I do really think that Aggie is the funniest child I ever knew!"

"Eh?" asked the earl, rousing himself violently.

"Aggie writes such nonsense," said Bertha, a little flatly. She had half expected to find her husband unsympathetic, yet she was already sorry that she had spoken.

"Nonsense, does she?" he repeated vaguely. "What sort of nonsense?"

"Oh, it wouldn't interest you; of course it

is only silly tittle-tattle, and things that amuse us, Aggie and me."

"I think I like the things that amuse you," said the earl gently; "suppose you tell me part of her letter, dear?"

Bertha picked up some of the scattered pages, and sorted a few, and turned over others. No portion of Aggie's long letter seemed sufficiently well suited for Lord Delachaine's edification. "What a pity," thought the elder sister, "what a sad pity that I did not have the poor dear better grounded in grammar!" Presently, however, she took heart of grace, and began to read in a low voice :

"'I am becoming quite a milliner; you have no idea, my dearest loveliest old Booffles'— that's me, you know," put in Bertha shyly—"'what a transcendental kind of cap this I myself has made for Mrs. Weagles. It fits her like the coiffure of

Fortunatus, though I don't fancy he had mauve ribbons. Susan says it's " hexquisite !" ' "

" Ah !" enunciated the earl, drawing a long breath. " Is Mrs. Weagles quite—quite the sort of companion fitted for your sister, do you think, Bertha, my dear ? "

" She's very good and kind," said Bertha, hurriedly trying to find another tolerably appropriate passage :

" ' It rains cats and dogs, and when it doesn't it's as cold as cold ! ' "

This was harmless enough, certainly, but the remark was followed by others, less impersonal, into which Bertha nearly floundered. But she saved herself by what seemed at first a really creditable extract :

" ' Mrs. Weagles' son's boy, who's at school, and quite big now, has got some delightful books up in his bedroom—some of them were Mrs. Weagles' own son's before. There's a lovely old-fashioned comic latin grammar in which it says :

> Musa, Musæ,
> The gods are at tea,

and, do you know, Booffles darling, whenever I see that, I think of you and your earl sitting opposite to each other like ninepins, having nothing to say, and looking amiably at each other across your dignified table.'"

There was a dreadful pause.

"Mightn't I read the letter myself ? " asked the earl slowly. "Surely, my love, now that you are my wife, everything concerning your sister is of importance and interest to me."

"Ye—es," answered Bertha, reddening, and feeling as guilty as innocent people are apt to do. If it had only not been for several reprehensible passages ! Besides, was it not a bargain between herself and Aggie that their letters should be sacred? It had never occurred to Bertha that Lord Delachaine would enquire into her sister's childish prattle, whilst it seemed the one privilege left to the poor child to write whatever floated through her foolish mind.

"You see," said Bertha timidly, "you see, dear John, Aggie has been used to chatter in such a *very* silly way to me."

"My dearest, do you think I cannot make allowances?" returned Lord Delachaine, stretching out his hand for the letter.

Poor Bertha hastily piled the sheets together in proper order. There were such a lot of them—it seemed as if they never would come right! Meanwhile, a hopeful thought crossed her mind that the earl, having but slight knowledge of Aggie's character and notions, might consider the allusion to the gods a flattering one.

"Thank you, my love," said Lord Delachaine, possessing himself of the bundle. At this moment Giusti re-entered the room.

" I tink, Milor," said the irrepressible courier, "dat peut-être Miladi and Milor vould vish to know here is a festa to-night. Piccola—de gondoliers dey sing and ornament de gondolas vid lanternes chinoises— Milor have heard, perhaps. Ven dere are family inglese in de hotel, dey try to get up little festa."

" Yes, thank you," said the earl indifferently.

" If Miladi have not seen before, it is quite nécessaire to go. It vil be pretty sight— tout-à-fait bellissima."

" Thank you, Giusti," repeated the earl.

" Milor pardon dat I mention ? " continued Giusti, gesticulating with his ringed hands, and unwilling to depart.

" Oh, certainly. You can think about it,

Bertha, and do as you like. Will you dress now, dear, and let us take a little turn in the Piazza ?"

Bertha went gladly. She was on thorns whilst Aggie's letter lay in her husband's hand. She could not but feel guilty of a kind of betrayal towards the child, and this feeling made her uncomfortable. Still, she argued, she could not have withheld the letter ; in truth, it was not easy to withstand Lord Delachaine. A man of quiet concentrated mind—accustomed, moreover, to command others during the better part of sixty years—is likely to impress those about him with a tolerable idea of justifiable supremacy. Lord Delachaine was unused to the society of young women, and was perhaps imbued with old-fashioned notions of wifely obedience. It certainly would never have occurred to him that Bertha was likely to refuse any ordinary request of his, couched in the polite and dignified language that he was accustomed to adopt.

Bertha occupied a long while in dressing, exchanging her tea-gown for plain walking attire. During this time, Lord Delachaine waded successfully enough through poor Aggie's lengthy scrawl. One sentence therein disturbed him considerably, but it was none of those on which Bertha's anxiety had fixed; for, if Lord Delachaine's serenity was clouded, it was entirely owing to the following words. Lightly written as they were, they remained engraven in his mind, ready to torment and torture him on every available occasion.

"I met Dr. Jackson in the street yesterday," thus wrote Aggie. "He looked so ill—quite different. I don't think he takes care of himself. He asked about you, and then he went off in a great hurry."

"Now I am ready," said Bertha's voice

cheerily, as she came back into the sitting-room.

Side by side the newly-wedded pair strolled through Venice, visiting several places of interest. Lord Delachaine conscientiously carried Murray's handbook, whilst Bertha studied Baedeker. Had she followed her own inclination, she would have cared for neither the verification of historical facts, nor the analysis of pictorial effects. Her mind wanted to drink in the lovely scene before her senselessly, vaguely. She longed for Aggie, for her old friend Eldon, for some one not so painstaking and yet so cruelly unappreciative as her husband.

She was not even sure but that his chief wish was to renovate the drainage of Venice, to provide its inhabitants with wholesome cheap food, to take down the sacred pictures from the churches, and to widen and repave a goodly number of the streets !

With the audacity of English travellers, Lord and Lady Delachaine wandered down some of the exceedingly narrow and dark *calli*—fit localities for blood-curdling murders, pathways curiously one like the other, leading into apparently similar open spaces or fondamenti, or perpetually crossing canals by means of the very same kind of narrow bridges, from which other *calli* wind away yet further into the mysterious heart of the water city, away from all recognizable boundaries or landmarks.

In vain did the earl make enquiries for the whereabouts of Danieli's hotel. A number of little ragged urchins simultaneously explained. They spoke volubly, and of course unintelligibly. Then a number of elderly unkempt females and slatternly girls stretched out their gaunt arms in what seemed to the strangers to be the most bewildering directions. It was quite dark when the hotel was

finally reached; by that time a dozen guides
of different ages and sizes were walking in
single file in front of tired Bertha and her
husband.

If the earl, during the greater part of the
expedition, had been somewhat more silent
than usual, this had passed unnoticed by
Bertha, to whom the very novel and picturesque sights and sounds were a keen
delight and satisfaction, especially since she
had slipped the Baedeker into her pocket.
Lord Delachaine was however dissatisfied,
and that chiefly with himself.

He was truly annoyed that he had asked
to read Aggie's letter. He had done so in
honesty and singleness of purpose; partly
with a wish to know more of the child, in
order that he might help hereafter with her
education, especially to influence her in a
right way; partly, also, it must be confessed,
because his mind was disturbed and ill at

ease, and he had scarcely known what he was asking. Now, he blamed himself for having, as he considered, played the spy. If, on glancing through Aggie's epistle, the thought had lightly crossed his mind that he might gain some knowledge which would calm his doubts—if indeed he admitted doubts for the future—he had not put such a thought into words, even to himself, and so it had not weighed with him. He had certainly expected to find nothing but the merest childish nonsense in Aggie's letter, and yet now, as he reflected, he was justly punished for what was not such allowable curiosity as it had first seemed! Moreover, the sentence he had read and re-read, and which had stung as well as pained him, held a sting none the less sharp because it in some measure repeated the wound he had just before received from the anonymous letter. Still, he would not confess to that wound;

no, he must not. He would assuredly never
confess it to Bertha. It were nothing short
of an insult to that young, fair, gentle wife
of his if he but breathed a suspicion of her,
even to herself. Was not mutual trust the
first thing, ay, the most priceless thing in
married life ? Perchance, thought the earl
as he revolved this terrible question, perchance he might have enquired from Bertha
regarding Dr. Jackson had he not foolishly
asked to see the child's letter. Now by his
impetuosity he had placed himself in a
position in which it would be utter meanness
to demand explanations. He could not take
advantage of a child's frankness, to say
nothing of his wife's yielding amiability !

When evening came, and Lord and Lady
Delachaine sallied forth in their gondola, the
earl's thoughts ran mostly in the same miserable strain as before. He sought to conceal
his recurring vexation ; he treated his wife

with the attentive courtesy that characterized him; he even tried to make pleasant starts of conversation for her. As the gondola glided swiftly over the dark water, he came to a distinct resolution that he would forget both the evil words he had perused, and the miserable thoughts that had arisen within him; he registered a mental vow that he would trust Bertha "all in all."

The gondola, together with several other gondolas, followed the lighted open boats which conveyed the musicians. Some of these latter played upon violins, others upon harps, mandolines, or guitars. Many singers, also, were closely packed side by side in these boats, and from under strings of gaily-coloured Chinese lanterns, they trilled out (with full rich southern voices that reached far beyond the grand canal) popular melodies, the words of which some of their listeners could perhaps not understand, but which suggested, from the very first bars, the emotion of beauty and poetry, and nature's wondrous harmony.

Then the moon, like a goddess invoked, came forth from behind a bank of clouds, irradiating the whole scene, and casting a broad silver pathway on the water, whilst the great palaces on either side stood out against the shimmering sky, silent and dark in their strong shadowing. The music rose and fell; the dense floating mass of gondolas increased in volume with every inlet of the canal. Some red and green Bengal lights flashed out here and there, with long trailing reflections, revealing the architecture of great water-gates, and iron trellised windows, from which came the sight of merry faces, and the sound of joyous voices. At last the Rialto was reached, and there, under the echoing bridge, the gaily-decked music-boats paused with their rocking lanterns, and around them pressed the attendant black gondolas. "Santa Lucia," sang an unaccompanied quartett, beginning the well-known melody that is as much loved in Venice as at Naples:

"Sul mare luccica
L'astro d'argento,
Placida è l'onda,
Prospero è il vento,"

and, like a triumphant wave of joy, from all sides burst a mighty chorus.

The earl had taken from the breast-pocket of his coat a small thin letter; he tore it slowly and deliberately into innumerable fragments, which he tossed over the side of the gondola. The tiny pieces floated away amongst the sombre eddies.

"What's that?" asked Bertha; "what are you tearing up, John?"

"Only a foolish note," said the earl gently. "It came to me to-day; it is nothing of any consequence—nothing that I mind in the very least."

"Oh listen!" exclaimed Bertha. Tears of sweet emotion were standing in her pretty eyes. They glistened in the moonlight. A spasm of delicious pain contracted her throat; she could not speak. The men were all singing again; this was a new song. Now came a girl's lovely voice rising high in the air like a nightingale's lament. Several of the people in the gondolas and sandolos around caught up the strain. It was a wild weird melody, something between a volkslied and a national hymn, and at the end, with a sort of strange exultation, the manly chorus shouted :

"Andiam ! Andiam !"

"Andiam," sighed a far-away voice lower down the canal, and then on different notes echoed the wild jubilant refrain ; it was here, there, and everywhere, sobbing, murmuring, triumphing out into the night ; like a will-o'-the-wisp it seemed to impel the listener to set off ardently, he knew not whither.

Suddenly, there was silence; a thrill of motion made the crowded gondolas shiver. A few had begun to move away with a slight — a very slight — plashing of oars. The charm was broken; people whispered and talked ; the gondoliers swore softly ; some good-humoured strangers laughed.

"Oh, it is grand, very grand ! " cried Bertha, with a deep-drawn sigh. She longed to weep, she knew not wherefore. Turning to her husband, she repeated excitedly :

" Isn't it fine, John ? "

" Yes, it is very beautiful," answered the earl quietly. He put out his arm and placed it round Bertha's waist, and, drawing her towards him, he kissed her softly on the forehead.

END OF VOL. I.

PRINTED BY WILLIAM CLOWES AND SONS, LIMITED,
LONDON AND BECCLES.   *J. D. & Co.*

www.ingramcontent.com/pod-product-compliance
Lightning Source LLC
Chambersburg PA
CBHW020844020726
47497CB00005B/1247